JOURNEY TO ATLANTIS

BOOKS BY PHILIP ROY

Seas of South Africa (2013)

Me & Mr. Bell (2013)

Outlaw in India (2012)

Blood Brothers in Louisbourg (2012)

Ghosts of the Pacific (2011)

River Odyssey (2010)

Journey to Atlantis (2009)

Submarine Outlaw (2008)

JOURNEY TO ATLANTIS

THE SUBMARINE OUTLAW SERIES

PHILIP ROY

RONSDALE PRESS

JOURNEY TO ATLANTIS
Copyright © 2009 Philip Roy
Second Printing June 2013

RONSDALE PRESS
3350 West 21st Avenue, Vancouver, B.C., Canada V6S 1G7
www.ronsdalepress.com

Typesetting: Julie Cochrane, in Minion 12 pt on 16
Cover Art & Design: Nancy de Brouwer, Alofli Graphic Design
Paper: Ancient Forest Friendly "Silva" (FSC) — 100% post-consumer waste,
    totally chlorine-free and acid-free

Ronsdale Press wishes to thank the following for their support of its publishing program: the Canada Council for the Arts, the Government of Canada through the Book Publishing Industry Development Program (BPIDP), the British Columbia Arts Council, and the Province of British Columbia through the British Columbia Book Publishing Tax Credit program.

Library and Archives Canada Cataloguing in Publication

Roy, Philip, 1960–
    Journey to Atlantis / Philip Roy.

(The submarine outlaw series)
ISBN 978-1-55380-076-7 (print)
ISBN 978-1-55380-074-3 (ebook) / 978-1-55380-196-2 (pdf)

    I. Title. II. Series: Roy, Philip, 1960– .
The submarine outlaw series.

PS8635.O91144J69 2009   jC813'.6   C2009-902165-X

At Ronsdale Press we are committed to protecting the environment. To this end we are working with Markets Initiative (www.oldgrowthfree.com) and printers to phase out our use of paper produced from ancient forests. This book is one step towards that goal.

Printed in Canada by Marquis Printing, Montreal, Quebec

for Peter

ACKNOWLEDGEMENTS

Many sincere thanks to Ron and Veronica Hatch for consistently holding the bar high and making me work harder all the time. It is a much better book than it ever would have been without their careful scrutiny and suggestions. Thanks also to my wife Leila (and furry Fritzi), and to the unmatchable Julia, Peter and Thomas, the jewels of my life. Thanks to dear friends, Chris, Natasha, and Chiara; to my sister, Angela; and to my darling mother, Ellen, for putting up with my hissy fits and all.

Chapter One

THE LEGEND IS ANCIENT.

Thirty-five hundred years ago the sea swallowed a rich and powerful island. It dragged it down to the bottom with everyone and everything in it. All of it disappeared in a single day, without a trace. Now everyone wonders if it ever really existed. The thing is, people have never stopped talking about it. That doesn't make sense. Why would people talk about something for so long if it never existed? So I figured it probably did. Then I thought, well . . . maybe I could find it.

I woke with a seagull on my stomach. When he saw me open my eyes he hopped from foot to foot and glared at me.

"What do you want, Seaweed?"

Hollie was on the bed too. He was chewing the rubber handle of a hammer into tiny soggy pieces. He must have been at it for hours. *This*, this feathered and furry pair, was my crew — a dog and a seagull. It had been a long winter in the boathouse and they were anxious to go to sea.

So was I.

I fed the crew and hurried downstairs. There, suspended in the air like a whale lifted out of an aquarium, was my submarine. Two days earlier, we had sprayed the final coat of a sophisticated, slippery paint that was supposed to reduce drag and make the sub five percent faster through the water. Ziegfried, master inventor and junkyard genius, was right about ninety-nine percent of the time. His latest obsession — to make the sub faster — had kept us hard at work all winter long. We had installed a bigger, more powerful diesel engine, more industrial batteries and a new propeller with aggressive torque. Now, with this shiny new blue-black coat of paint, and the dolphin-like nose that Ziegfried had welded to the front, the sub looked more like a sea mammal than a submarine. Today, just a few days after my fifteenth birthday, it would finally go back in the water. I was almost too excited.

But I had to tether that excitement. Nine times out of ten Ziegfried would find something else to test, and the re-launch would be set back once again. I had to calm the butterflies in my stomach and just hope it wouldn't happen today.

There were voices outside. Two doors slammed on the truck — Ziegfried, and my grandfather. When the ocean had frozen over in December, and the fishing boats were up on planks, my grandfather surprised us by coming out to the boathouse. He just showed up one day, without asking what he could do, and got busy. Pretty soon we didn't know how we had ever gotten along without him. More than once I witnessed Ziegfried, one of the biggest and strongest men in all of Newfoundland, reach over an impossibly sealed jar of glue to my grandfather, a much smaller man, but with larger hands, and he twisted off the top as if it were a toy. He handed the jar back and Ziegfried took it graciously. My grandfather never uttered a word when we were working. Ziegfried talked constantly, mumbling to himself mostly, as if he were thinking out loud. But the two men worked side by side harmoniously. And I was their assistant, running for tools, filing the edges of metal cuts, holding lights, making tea. Once the sub was back in the water, all of that would change. Then, I was the captain.

But I wasn't the captain yet. When they came inside, my grandfather immediately frowned at me, because I had just woken up and he was such an early riser. But I had learned that his frowns were not nearly as serious as they looked. In fact, I was beginning to understand that his severe bearing — looking so disapproving all the time — had nothing to do with me. That was just the way he was. I was used to sleeping in because I was nocturnal on the sub. So was the crew. My grandfather quickly scanned the boardwalk around the sub. Fortunately, I had remembered to sweep it clear before going to bed. He frowned again anyway. Ziegfried reached over and put his hand on one of the cables holding the sub up in the air and stared at the water beneath it. He took a deep breath and sighed. It was a sigh that spoke volumes. I imitated him exactly and waited anxiously to hear the words that came from his mouth.

"Well . . . I suppose . . ."

He paused. I held my breath.

"I suppose . . ."

"There's a storm coming," warned my grandfather.

Of the few times my grandfather chose to speak, I wished this hadn't been one of them.

"They didn't mention a storm on the radio," Ziegfried said respectfully.

"All the same," snapped my grandfather.

Ziegfried sighed again. The decision was his. As much as he respected my grandfather, he wouldn't be swayed by a fisherman's superstitious way of predicting the weather.

"I suppose she is ready for a run at sea. Why don't you sail her to Sheba's island? That'll take you two or three days. I can drive to the coast in the truck, take a boat over with supplies for the big voyage and meet you there. Then you can tell me how she's handling and whether she's ready for the journey. What do you say?"

I felt like yelling with excitement but didn't. I was standing in a boathouse with two of the most cautious people you were ever likely to meet in Newfoundland.

"That seems like a pretty good idea to me," I said, as calmly as possible. "Then, when we meet up at Sheba's, I can tell you how she's handling."

I knew that was just what he had said, but I was too excited to think of anything else to say.

We lowered the sub into the water and unleashed it from the cables. The newly painted hull glistened like a black jelly-bean. It was beautiful. I climbed inside, then heard a pitiful bark from the boardwalk, so I went back out, picked up Hollie and carried him in. Seaweed followed immediately, tapping his beak on the portal before dropping inside like a chimney sweep, as was his custom.

My sub was twenty feet long and eight feet high on the outside, with the portal jutting up another three feet. Inside was a different story. Standing up straight in the soft cedar and pine interior, I had barely two inches to spare. I used to have four, but had grown. With my arms outstretched I could just barely touch both walls with my fingertips. The oval shape of the hull, minus the wood and insulation, the mechanics beneath the floor and above the ceiling, plus the compartments in the stern, left me with an interior space a little short of fourteen feet by six. It was more than enough in which to stretch out but I had to duck my head in the bow and stern. Standing directly beneath the portal gave me a lot of extra headroom and the *feeling* of more space, which was particularly welcome when we were submerged for long periods of time. I also found a way to fit a bar across the inside of the portal to do chin-ups, and was pretty good at them now. And sometimes I would just hang there and swing.

Although we had replaced the engine and added new batteries, they were housed in separate, watertight compartments in the stern, and so the main area of the sub remained more or less the same as before. The stationary bike was still in the center, my hanging cot behind, and the control panel with sonar and radar screens in front. The periscope hung on the starboard side of the control panel. I had to turn sideways to pass it. The observation window, in the floor of the bow, was also the same, except that Hollie's beloved blanket, rather frayed at the edges, had been replaced by a lovely quilt my grandmother had knitted especially for him. Well, that didn't fly. Hollie picked up the new blanket in his teeth, carried it dutifully to the stern and dropped it in front of the door to the engine compartment, where his litter-box was kept. Then he whined at me until I went back into the loft, found his old blanket in a box and brought it back. He pawed it into a proper sleeping berth and plopped down on it. Seaweed settled on his usual spot on the opposite side of the observation window — sitting very still, like the Buddha — and watched the little dog fuss.

It didn't take long to load up for a three-day sail. I was ready in less than an hour. But Ziegfried felt the need to climb inside and go through a checklist with me. Inside the sub he had to crouch like a giant inside a bus.

"When you're at sea, Al, make sighting tests of your wake, will you? I want to know if any of the changes we've made cause her to sail less true. She won't be faster if she's cutting arcs through the water."

"Okay."

"Make the same tests submerged and watch your depth gauge closely. Check for any deviation either vertical or horizontal."

"Okay."

He frowned and rubbed his brow. "These are the tests we can't make until she's in the water."

"I know. Don't worry, I'll make them right away."

I was glad we couldn't make every test in the boathouse, or I'd never get to sea. He looked down the list.

"Fuel?"

"Good."

"Oil?"

"Good."

"Air?"

"Topped up."

"Water?"

"Same, . . . topped up."

"Food?"

"One week fresh; two weeks emergency."

Ziegfried knew all of this, but his cautious, exacting nature wouldn't permit him to skip steps. When he said a vessel was ready for sea, she was.

When we finished, I came outside and stood on the boardwalk beside the two men. There was never any way to thank them adequately for the gifts they had given me, both in their own ways, and yet I would feebly try. But they wouldn't hear of it.

"Bring back another treasure," Ziegfried said jokingly.

"I will!"

"There's a storm coming," repeated my grandfather, and shook his head. But he reached out and took my hand, completely concealing mine inside of his.

"Hold on," said my grandfather. "I've got something in the truck."

He went out and returned with a long wooden case. "I've been meaning to give you this for a while now."

He put the case down on the floor and opened it. My face dropped. So did Ziegfried's.

"It's a dangerous world out there. If you're going to go as far as I think you are, you might as well take this along. I don't need it anymore."

My grandfather lifted up a heavy long shotgun and handed it to me. I was so shocked I didn't know what to say. I had never even shot a gun before.

"Uhhh . . . thank-you, Grandpa. It's a wonderful gift."

"Oh, it's nothing. I have no need of it anymore, and who knows, you just might."

I thanked him again as graciously as I could, and they went out. A moment later, Ziegfried hurried back in by himself.

"I forgot something, Al," he said, and reached over and took the shotgun from my hands. "It's quite an honour for your grandfather to pass this on to you like that."

He stared at the shotgun in his hands, and a strange look came over his face. And then the gun just sort of slipped out of his hands and dropped into the water beside the sub. We both watched it disappear.

"Oh! What a shame!" said Ziegfried. "Oh, well, it's just as well, I suppose. It was kind of an old shotgun, I think. And one thing's for sure, Al, when there's a gun around, *some-body's* going to get shot. You have a great sail now. I'll see you at Sheba's in a few days."

I stood and watched him go. I needed time to think about what had just happened. It was not for no reason that I trusted him with my life.

It didn't surprise me that Ziegfried and my grandfather didn't hang around until we left. Their work was done. This was their way of letting me know I was on my own now, and that was important. If I needed anyone to help me get safely out to sea, then I had no business going out in the first place.

I climbed inside the sub, shut the hatch and let water into the ballast tanks. We started to dive. A shiver of excitement rushed through me. I engaged the batteries and felt the vibrations of the new propeller come up through the floor. The feeling was thrilling. I turned on the sonar and watched the screen closely as I steered the sub through the craggy rocks outside. It was one of the most isolated spots along the northern coast of Newfoundland. All the same, I motored a mile out from shore before surfacing. I never wanted anyone to know where the Submarine Outlaw was moored for the winter.

A mile out, we surfaced and I opened the hatch. Seaweed climbed the portal, took a look all around and jumped into the wind. What a familiar sight that was. I grinned. Hollie barked sharply from the bottom of the portal. I carried him up and we leaned against the open hatch and breathed in the fresh sea air. It was wonderful to be back at sea. There were a few clouds, a steady wind, but no sign of a storm in any direction. The weather report had made no mention of a storm. Strange. I wondered if my grandfather was getting too old to predict the weather.

He wasn't.

Chapter Two

❧

THE SUB *WAS* FASTER. I could tell just by the feel of it cutting through the water. It had more power, less resistance and the fastest nose in the sea. It wasn't exactly a dolphin, but three years ago it wasn't anything more than an old oil tank, until Ziegfried transformed it. Now, after two and a half years of genius, dedication and very hard work, it was a sleek-looking, sea-faring vessel with real power and stealth. I was very proud of it.

But speed is relative. The average sailboat can sail at about seven knots. One knot is one nautical mile per hour. A nautical mile is a little longer than a land mile — 1.15 times as far. A typical ocean freighter can sail at a maximum speed of about twenty knots, but would never do so because it would burn too much fuel, and that would be too expensive. Most sail at half that speed. Diesel-electric submarines, like those used in WWII, could reach up to twenty-five knots on the surface, but only half as much submerged. Modern nuclear powered submarines are much faster, reaching speeds of almost fifty knots under water! That's as fast as a hovercraft, or a car on the highway! Unbelievable! My sub's top speed was about fifteen knots on the surface, or used to be, and only half of that submerged.

But speed on the water is also complicated, and you have to do the math. If we were sailing at fifteen knots against a current of three knots, and there were large swells, and we were riding up and down the crests and troughs like a roller-coaster, and the wind was blowing against us, then our actual speed measured against land might be only six or seven knots. And if I were just pedalling the sub against a strong current, we might actually be going backwards without knowing it! On the other hand, if we were sailing *with* a current, with the wind on our back and following closely in the wake of another vessel, we could be sailing over twenty knots.

I made the sighting tests I promised to make. The sea was calm enough to reveal our wake for a quarter of a mile behind us. I fixed our course straight ahead, strapped on the harness and climbed out of the portal with a ruler in my hand. The wind blew my hair across my face. Raising the ruler to my eye, I held the edge of it against the line in the water and watched for any twists or turns. There were none. Our course was as true as an arrow.

Submerging, I made a similar test by watching the depth gauge, and, by following a sonar picture of the sea floor. There was no variation in our course whatsoever. Ziegfried would be happy to hear that.

We were submerged for a little more than an hour and I was surprised upon surfacing to discover that the wind had picked up quite a bit. It was blowing from the east, which was a little unusual. I checked the weather forecast again. Stronger winds were reported but still no mention of a storm. An hour later, the winds were stronger again and the waves were growing. It takes about two hours for a steady wind to shape large waves. I decided to call Ziegfried on the short wave to let him know the results of the sighting tests, but he was not answering. I climbed the portal and scanned the eastern horizon with binoculars. No storm in sight. Okay, but I was starting to feel a sense of something foreboding. I didn't know why. Was it just that my grandfather had predicted it?

To test our maximum speed I shut the engine and let the sub drift. Then, I measured our drift against a sonar picture of the sea floor. The current was two knots. Sailing with the current, but against the wind, I cranked up the engine all the way and watched the sonar screen as we plowed through the water. In no time we reached our old maximum speed of fifteen knots. Then . . . sixteen, seventeen eighteen . . . nineteen, twenty . . . twenty-one! We stayed at twenty-one knots for a few moments, then slowly pushed ahead . . . twenty-two . . . twenty-three! I rushed up the portal to look outside. At twenty-three knots the sub cut through the water like a shark. Waves splayed evenly on both sides of us. It was very exciting. I looked up in the sky to make sure that Seaweed was still following us. Yup. We'd have to sail a lot faster to outrun a flying seagull.

Subtracting two knots for the current, our new top speed was twenty-one knots. That was about the fastest I could ride my bicycle on a flat road. It also meant we were twenty-five percent faster than before. Ziegfried would be very pleased.

Now I had to test our underwater speed. But this time I wanted Seaweed inside. I waved a slice of bread in the air and he came racing out of the sky like a lightning bolt, hit the water beside the sub, hopped onto the hull and shook himself off. Then he jumped onto the hatch, grabbed the bread and dropped inside.

I took one last peek at the horizon and wondered if that were a gray mass I was seeing, or was it just my imagination. Staring long distances at sea could be mesmerizing. That's what sea birds were good at. Seaweed could tell the difference between a compass and a cookie from about half a mile away on a clear day. I sealed the hatch, flooded the tanks and we went down to one hundred feet, well below the surface current. I made a cup of tea, ate some cookies and fed the crew dog biscuits. It was an unbreakable rule on the sub —

you never ate alone. That would be the height of rudeness in the company of a dog and seagull.

There were only two ways to propel the sub when it was submerged: by battery and by pedalling; the volume of air needed by the engine made it impossible to run it under water. From a dead stop I engaged the batteries, sat at the sonar screen and tracked our course along the sea floor. The sub pushed steadily ahead towards its maximum submerged speed. It was a surprise! Sixteen knots! That was faster than our old surface speed. What that revealed was that the new nose and slippery paint made more of a difference than the new engine. I couldn't wait to tell Ziegfried. But I wanted to test my new pedalling speed first.

Ziegfried had connected the gears of an old touring bicycle to the driveshaft of the sub. Simply by pedalling the bike I could turn the propeller. But it wasn't very fast — about as fast as a canoe. The good thing was that it was quiet. The bike gears and driveshaft were so well greased there was virtually no sound while I was pedalling, which was important when we were trying to sneak away from ships that might be listening.

Now, since I was stronger than when the sub first went into the water a year ago, we had added five more gears to the bike. We had also attached a new propeller. I climbed onto the bike and started pedalling. I went through the old gears quickly and started on the new ones. It took all my strength and concentration but I stayed with it long enough to bring the sub to five knots. That was hard and I was sweating! Still, five knots was twice as fast as before — a big improvement. Anxious to tell Ziegfried, I surfaced once again to make the call but . . . the storm had arrived.

I listened to the radio.

"Environment Canada has issued severe weather warnings and advises all boaters to stay off the water until further notice . . ."

My grandfather was right. How he could have known before everyone else was a mystery to me. Oh well, the joy of a submarine was that you could submerge beneath a storm and not even know it was raging above you. There was just one thing I needed to check first. The radio continued.

". . . three fishing boats reported missing. The coastguard will initiate a search once the storm has abated . . ."

Shoot! It had already happened. Three fishing boats were lost. The coastguard couldn't look for them until the worst was over. By then it was usually too late. Could I do something to help, I wondered? I could sail into the heart of a storm. That's what a submarine was good for. I had done it before. But finding anything lost at sea was like walking into a desert with a metal-detector — you could search for days and days and find nothing.

And yet I had to try.

They had sailed from Deadman's Bay, the radio had said, but the storm would have carried them away. I knew the area and we were less than a day's sail away, so I plotted a course and engaged full battery power. It was unlikely I would find all three boats, but maybe if I was lucky I could find one.

Thirteen hours later I did. And it was worse than I expected.

Chapter Three

THERE WERE TWO OF them in the boat. They were huddled together and had tied themselves down. They must have thrown overboard everything they could, trying to make the boat as buoyant as possible. It seemed to have worked because the boat refused to sink even though it was filled with water. One of them was holding onto the other, who appeared lifeless. And he was.

I saw the arm of the other man go up when I drew near. He was weak. The storm rammed the sub and fishing boat together several times, but there was nothing I could do about that. I kept myself strapped to the harness and threw the lifebuoy with all my strength. But it was futile. There was too much movement to make a decent toss and the surviving sailor was too weak to untie himself anyway.

I went back inside and grabbed more rope. If he couldn't come in, I would have to go out. If I left the hatch open the sub would swamp and sink, although the automatic switch would shut the hatch, and, after the sump pumps had removed enough water, about fifteen minutes or so, the sub would resurface. But if I were tied to the sub when it went down, I would drown. If I weren't tied to it, I would probably lose the sub anyway because the storm would carry it away. So . . . I had to go out on a rope *and* shut the hatch behind me. Not the nicest feeling.

I had never seen a dead body before, and I felt a little sick, but there was no time to think about that, only to reach out, cut the live man free, fit the lifebuoy over him and pull him to the sub. Once we were there, I'd open the hatch and help him inside. That was my plan. I only wished it could have been as simple as that.

I tied one end of the rope to a handle on the portal, climbed out with the lifebuoy and shut the hatch. A wave crashed over me immediately and I had to hold my breath. I could not understand how the man in the fishing boat had survived so long. Jumping into the boat, which was filled with water, I kept my eyes on the rope's slackness. If the waves pulled our two vessels apart, the rope would pull me out of the boat. I had to act quickly.

"I have to cut you free!" I yelled to the man. "Do you understand?"

He stared at me and raised his arm weakly. I didn't think he could speak. I nodded my head.

"I'm going to cut you free!"

Though the two of them were tied together, he had one arm wrapped tightly around the neck of his companion. I knew he was dead because of the way he was lying; I could just tell. The only thing that mattered to me was keeping the other man alive. What difference did a storm make to a dead man? Nor did I care if the body was left at sea. But the man I was rescuing did. When I cut him free of the ropes and fitted the lifebuoy over his head I couldn't pull his arm free of his companion.

"Let go!" I shouted. "We have to go . . . now!"

But he wouldn't. He looked up at me and I saw the terrible sadness in his eyes. I felt so badly for him, I really did, but I also knew we had to leave immediately. The rope had grown taut and the sub was about to pull me away any second.

"I'm sorry!" I yelled, and did what I had to do — the same thing rescuers have to do whenever they are grabbed by a panicking victim — I punched the man's arm, knocked it free and shoved the lifebuoy over him. He tried to struggle against me but was too weak. The sub pulled away and yanked the two of us out of the boat. I heard him crying.

"It's okay!" I shouted. "I will come back for him!"

I couldn't believe I had said that. The thought of pulling a dead body into the sub did not appeal to me. I just felt so badly for him.

He had no strength at all. The waves pulled us under several times and he went limp. But he was still conscious when I pulled us close enough to grab hold of the sub railing. It was too difficult for me. All I wanted was to get inside, submerge and catch my breath. Getting the hatch open was okay, but getting him inside was almost impossible. He didn't have the use of his limbs at all, and I had to do everything. Then, once I had him in the portal, he slipped. I saw him fall down inside and I felt awful. I was trying as hard as I could but he was bigger than I was and a lot heavier. I jumped inside, pulled him away from the water rushing inside and put a pillow under his head. He was still conscious. He was trying to say something.

"Please . . ."

"What? What is it?"

"Please . . . my brother . . ."

I nodded.

"Yes. I will. I promise. Just wait here."

So I went back out. I tied a longer length of rope, jumped into the sea and swam over to the boat. It didn't bother me too much to see the body now; I was just so busy. I cut the ropes and pushed the lifebuoy down over his head and shoulders, then tied the sub rope that ran through my harness to the lifebuoy. I didn't feel strong enough to carry him back to the sub, so I pulled him behind me. But he started to sink. If the sub hadn't been pitching to the side I would never have been able to pull him up. The hardest thing of all was sliding his body in, feet first, then the arms, and then the head. I lowered him inside with the rope wrapped around the portal, dropping him a little at a time. Then I jumped in, shut the hatch, staggered over to the controls and dove to one hundred feet. I was breathing so hard I was seeing black spots. My back ached. My arms ached. My hands were full of rope burns. Now I had two passengers in my sub, and one of them was dead.

The live man started throwing up. I hurried over and turned his head so that he wouldn't drown in his own vomit. Pools of water came up with his vomit. It didn't surprise me that he had swallowed a lot of seawater. Probably it was in his lungs too. He needed medical attention immediately. All I could do was run for the coast as quickly as possible. But we had to come in submerged; I didn't think any of us could take any more of the storm. It was probably the fastest way anyway, with all the tossing and pitching of the waves. Why hadn't I believed my grandfather? But then, if I had, *both* of these men would be dead.

I covered him with blankets and made him as comfortable as I could, then turned my attention to the crew. Hollie seemed nervous having passengers on board so I let him sit on my lap and nibble on dog biscuits. After a while I turned and saw Seaweed standing on the dead man.

"Get off, Seaweed!" I said, but he just stared at me. I figured that seagulls were pretty comfortable around drowned bodies.

We were about two hours away from the coast, I calculated. The storm was too bad to rendezvous with the coastguard, unless I met them somewhere in a sheltered bay, which would likely be too far away anyway. I figured I could contact the RCMP by shortwave and ask them to bring an ambulance. But where would I meet them? In the storm it was almost impossible to know where we were coming in.

When I guessed we were about an hour from land, I surfaced, turned on the radio and made the call. The storm hadn't lessened at all and my passengers were rolling around on the floor. The radio was full of static. I didn't know how to identify myself except by the name everyone had given me the year before.

"This is the Submarine Outlaw. I am requesting an ambulance for two fishermen. One of them is dead. Over."

". . . RCMP . . . repeat . . . message please . . . identify . . . position . . ."

"This is the Submarine Outlaw. I have two victims from the storm. I think I'm coming in around Cape Freels. I'm not sure. I expect one hour. Over."

". . . submarine . . . land? . . . ambulance . . . storm . . . Over."

"Can you set up a spotlight? I can read Morse code. Over."

"Roger . . . spotlight . . . ambulance . . . how many dead? Over."

"Two victims. One of them is dead. Over."

As we approached land I caught glimpses of lights but none of them blinking in code. Were we too far north, or south? Looking at my charts I guessed south. So, turning north, and against all my experience as a submariner, I turned on the sub's bright floodlights, aimed them towards shore and went up the coast hoping the authorities would spot us.

Half an hour later they did. The RCMP met us in a sheltered cove with a motorized inflatable boat. Even though the cove was sheltered, the sea tossed everything around like rain in a bucket. I saw four vehicles with lights on above the dock. Three officers motored out to meet us. They were wearing bright orange sea jackets and carrying a megaphone: two men and one woman. One man waved while the lady spoke through the megaphone.

"Are there injured?" she said.

I nodded and raised one hand.

"Dead?" she asked.

I nodded again and raised the other hand. As the boat approached the sub I noticed the lady was young and looked kind of nervous. One of the men smiled when I reached down to help him up the side of the sub.

"So *you're* the Submarine Outlaw?" he said.

He looked at the sub and shook his head. He didn't seem too interested in the fact that I was carrying wounded and dead passengers.

"It's pretty small," he said. "You go to sea in *this*?"

"Yup."

I was nervous because I knew my submarine wasn't legal. What if they told me to moor it right then and there to the dock? What would I do? I just hoped they wouldn't say anything. Suddenly, the expression on his face changed.

"Okay, son. Show us your cargo."

"Umm . . . we won't all fit inside," I said. "And they're too heavy for me to carry out by myself. We need to use a harness and rope."

I held up my harness.

"No," he said, "you better let me have a look."

"Okay."

I held onto the hatch and exchanged a nervous smile with the lady in the boat while her partner climbed inside and took a look. When he poked his head out he made a couple of hand signals to the officers in the boat and the lady spoke into her radio.

The transfer of the victims seemed to take forever. They had to be lifted out by stretcher, one at a time. The injured man went first. I didn't believe they would ever get the stretcher through the portal but they did. They took him to shore and put him in the ambulance and it left immediately. Then, they came back for the dead man. The critical moment for me was when they took him away and were off the sub. That was my chance to leave. No one had asked me to stay or told me to report anywhere. I watched as the police van left. Then the three officers returned to their boat and headed out towards me. Yikes! So far I hadn't done anything illegal. But what if they told me to surrender my sub right then and there? What if I refused? Suddenly I felt frantic. I hated to leave like that, especially when they had been friendly to me, but I couldn't risk losing my sub. I stared at the approaching police boat. One man raised his hand and waved, gesturing for me to wait. I raised my arm awkwardly and waved in a friendly way, to say goodbye. Then I climbed inside, shut the hatch, slipped beneath the surface and disappeared.

Chapter Four

⚮

SHEBA'S ISLAND WASN'T much bigger than a soccer field. It was just a rock really, jutting out of the ocean at the end of a chain of tiny islands in Bonavista Bay. It had a hidden cove on the mainland side, where I could tie up the sub out of sight. The other side faced the stormy Atlantic. Her cottage was protected from the wind and sea on three sides by rock. The open side, all windows, gave her a spectacular view of the sunrise, and, according to her, of ghost ships, mermaids, dead sailors and other fantastic creatures from the deep. In truth, she had never claimed to see mermaids in Newfoundland, only to hear them.

Sheba was the friendliest and most interesting person I

had ever met and I loved visiting her. She was tall and lean and had long bright red hair that fell over her shoulders and all the way down her back in tiny, shell-like curls. She wore brightly coloured dresses and lots of jewellery. She looked directly into your eyes when she spoke, and her eyes, as green as a cat's, sparkled with joy. If there were such things as friendly witches who used magic for good purposes, that's what Sheba would be. And maybe she was; I was never really sure. She lived with about three dozen animals — dogs, cats, birds, goats, lizards and snakes. It was a zoo. They made a fuss over you at first, but settled down after a while. So long as you didn't mind sitting with a cockatiel on your shoulder, a cat on your lap and a goat nipping at your hair, you wouldn't even know they were there.

Living in a place hidden in fog a good part of the time, Sheba had created a miraculous system of lights that brought sunshine inside her cottage on the darkest days. Her kitchen was an indoor hydroponics garden, year-round. She grew tomatoes, peppers, onions, oranges, lemons, spinach, mushrooms, garlic, herbs, flowers and all kinds of things I had never heard of before that she put in her teas. She made mysterious teas that affected your moods. You never really knew what to expect and she wouldn't tell you.

I moored the sub to the rock, climbed out with Hollie and waved to Seaweed, who stayed on the bow. There was too much "society" on Sheba's island for Seaweed.

"Keep an eye on the sub, Seaweed."

Sheba looked greatly relieved when she saw me.

"Oh! Alfred! Thank Heavens you're all right!"

She threw her arms around me and hugged me. She was about half a foot taller than I was.

"Hi, Sheba. Of course I'm all right. Why wouldn't I be?"

"Because I read your cards two nights ago and they said you would be in danger yesterday. Were you in danger yesterday?"

"Well . . ."

"You were! I knew it! But you are all right now?"

"Yes. I'm fine."

"Good!"

She slapped her hands together. "Come in and have tea. Watch your step. Ziegfried is still making repairs. He will be here tomorrow. Oh, Alfred, I am so happy! My two men will be here at the same time once again!"

I liked the way she referred to us as her "men." Sheba always treated me as a full-grown man.

The tea had a licorice smell. A goat with sad eyes sniffed at the corner of the wood stove and was about to singe his whiskers.

"Edgar!" said Sheba. "This tea is not for you."

Edgar looked at me. I shrugged. Sheba sat down opposite me, took my hands in hers and looked deeply into my eyes.

"So. Tell me what happened."

"I don't know . . . It started two days ago with a strange feeling."

"A premonition?"

"Maybe. It was a dark feeling."

"Like something terrible was about to happen?"

"Yes. Sort of."

"Good. You must learn to trust those feelings."

She poured the tea. I had learned to drink her teas without milk. Don't curdle the passion of a flower with the discharge of a cow's stomach, she had said.

"When we surfaced, there was a really bad storm."

"I know! The worst storm in years. And then?"

"Well, the radio said there were three fishing boats lost."

"So, you went out to look for them."

"Yes. But two of them were already sunk."

"How did you know?"

"I found them later, on sonar."

"At the bottom?"

"No. One was at two hundred feet, the other at seventy-five. They were drifting down slowly."

"Horrible! And then?"

"I found two men in the other boat."

"Alive?"

"One of them . . . one of them . . ."

I felt a heaviness in my chest. Emotion rushed through me and my eyes started to water. I covered my face.

"Oh, Alfred! Let your tears fall. It's good for you. Tears are rain from the heart. You must let your heart rain free or the rest of your body will dry up and wither."

I wiped my eyes.

"It's embarrassing. I never cry."

"Of course you do! Everybody does. Ziegfried cries every time he sees a new kitten."

I laughed. It was true. Ziegfried cried as easily as a little girl. I wiped my cheeks and continued.

"I didn't realize I was so upset about it."

"Of course! It is *terribly* upsetting! So, one of them was alive and one wasn't?"

Every time I tried to speak, my chest got that heavy feeling and my eyes started. I took a deep breath. I noticed Sheba was crying along with me. She cried a lot too.

"He . . . he told me they were brothers."

She held my hands again and gently shook them.

"And you were able only to save one of them. Is that what is bothering you?"

I took another deep breath. My chest started to calm down.

"I just wish I had been able to get there sooner. I was too late to save them both. He cried when I pulled him away from his brother."

"Oh, Alfred. It is so awful, but you saved his life!"

"I know. I just felt so bad having to separate them."

"So you left the dead brother at sea?"

"No. I promised I would take him too, so I went back."

"Did you put him in your submarine and carry him to shore too?"

"Yes."

"Oh, Alfred! That was very brave! Now his ghost will not haunt the sea."

I took a drink of my tea. It filled my mouth with licorice flavour and my mind drifted away to images of a forest, dark and misty, a forest I had never even seen before. It was peaceful but mysterious. Everything about Sheba was peaceful and mysterious.

"But tell me now what you want to do, Alfred. Where do you want to go next?"

"I want to explore."

"Explore what?"

"Well . . ."

"Yes?"

"There's something I want to look for."

"And that is . . . ?"

"It might sound silly because it probably doesn't exist."

Sheba looked so deeply into my eyes I felt like she could read my mind.

"Try me."

Well, if I couldn't tell Sheba, who *could* I tell?

"I want to look for Atlantis. But I know it probably doesn't exist."

She sat up straight and her face broke into a beaming smile.

"That's perfect!"

"Do you think so?"

"It is so perfect, Alfred. For thousands of years people have been waiting for someone to find Atlantis again, and now, you are the one to do it. I am so happy!"

"But I'm not even sure it really exists. It might be just a myth."

"Of course it exists! It's waiting for you and your submarine to find it. Nobody has been able to find it because they didn't have the means that you have, or the determination. It is your destiny. Oh, Alfred, what a wonderful destiny you have."

I couldn't help smiling from ear to ear. "Well, Jacques Cousteau looked for it with a submersible."

"Did he *live* in his submarine? Did he travel around the world in it the way you do?"

"No."

"Well?"

Sheba was great. How wonderful to know someone like her.

Chapter Five

THE COTTAGE SHOOK beneath Ziegfried's feet. He came in with a water tank on one shoulder and a crate of fruit on the other. He also brought sacks of dog food, birdseed, canned food, flour, sugar, honey, raisins, soap, diesel fuel, and many other things necessary for an Atlantic crossing. Ziegfried already knew about my plans to look for Atlantis and he agreed wholeheartedly with Sheba, although he was inclined to agree with her about pretty much anything. He worshiped the ground on which she walked.

"Where there's smoke, Al, there's fire," he said. "Atlantis sure left a lot of smoke."

He never said he believed it existed, only that it would be

worthwhile to search for it. I didn't think he believed in mermaids either, but he wouldn't contradict Sheba, who was absolutely certain they existed.

"But Al, you were on the news again. They said you brought in two sailors. Is that true?"

I nodded.

"And only one of them was alive?"

I nodded again. I was afraid he was going to ask me a lot of questions and get me tearful again. It was bad enough in front of Sheba.

"So, you carried a dead body in the sub, then?"

I nodded once more. Then Sheba rescued me.

"Okay, you two, this pot of stew will not get eaten by itself. Neither will these fresh scones."

"Heavens Above!" said Ziegfried. "Fresh scones! We must have done something right somewhere along the line."

He put his hand on my shoulder as he passed.

"You are the bravest man I've ever known, Alfred. That's the God's honest truth."

I shrugged. Seemed to me it took less courage to bring the sailors in than it did to talk about it.

While Ziegfried worked on repairs to the cottage I read maps, charts and books. My plan was to sail straight across the Atlantic, stop at the Azores along the way, then turn south when I reached the coast of Portugal. I would sail as far south as Gibraltar, then enter the Mediterranean Sea from there. Once on the Mediterranean, I would explore in earnest, especially around the Greek islands, although the Azores was also one of the places legend suggested might have been the site of Atlantis. So was North America, though I had a hard time imagining Atlantis off the coast of Newfoundland. Sheba didn't.

"The Renaissance started," Sheba said, "when people began digging in their own backyards."

I looked at Ziegfried. He nodded like a child.

"Yah, but that was Italy," I said, "not Newfoundland."

"You never really know, Al," said Ziegfried, "until you look. What do your exploring instincts say?"

That was a good point. I would have to think about that. Having grown up in Dark Cove, a tiny fishing community, I had learned that everything exciting always happened somewhere else, and usually pretty far away. If I was following Atlantis' smoke, there certainly wasn't much of it in Newfoundland. True, the Vikings probably landed here, and buried dead sailors here. Some people claimed that the Irish came too. But that was all thousands of years after Atlantis disappeared. Besides, you couldn't very well dig up your backyard when your backyard was nothing but rock. My exploring instincts told me to get out into the ocean in my submarine and go somewhere else.

We would carry about three months of supplies with us and pick up more as we went along. Ziegfried and I planned to meet up in a couple of months, somewhere warm. We were thinking maybe Crete. He said he had always wanted to go to Greece.

And so I was busy poring over maps and charts and books on ocean currents and the topography of the sea. There were also history and geography books to examine because there were specific things to look for, such as sunken ships, treasure, submerged temples, and of course, sunken cities. I pored over the books with a passion that surprised even Ziegfried.

"Boy, if your history teacher could see you now, Al, eh?"

I raised my head out of a book. "I'm not *studying*. I'm just searching for stuff. These books are clues."

"I don't know," he said with a grin. "Some people might say it's the same thing."

"It isn't."

"Okay. If you say so. By the way, who *were* those people who lived on Crete before the Greeks?"

"The Minoans."

"Were they the ones who worshiped the bull and created that crazy maze?"

"Yup."

"Oh. Okay, thanks, Al. It's nice to hear from somebody who knows."

"I'm not studying."

"I know."

Ziegfried wanted to talk about the storm after Sheba went to bed. That didn't surprise me; drowning was probably the only thing he was afraid of. We spoke in hushed voices as we settled in our sleeping bags in front of the bay window. Hollie made himself cozy on my feet. The room was spread with cats and dogs, but over the course of the night they collected on and around the sleeping bags, most of them on Ziegfried. The goats stayed outside, as did Seaweed, the toughest of all.

"How did the sub handle in the storm?" Ziegfried asked.

"Great. The changes are amazing. She's quite a bit faster."

"How much?"

"Twenty-one knots."

"Fantastic. Under water?"

"Sixteen."

"Really?"

"Yup."

"And the bike?"

"Five knots, flat out."

"Fair enough. What about your wake?"

"Perfectly true."

"Good. And the engine . . . noisier?"

"Yah, a little, but I don't mind. It feels safer."

I knew that was what he wanted to hear.

"Good. Good."

He paused.

"Did you take in much water then?"

"Yah . . . quite a bit. The sump pumps worked great though. All my stuff stayed dry."

"Good."

Another pause.

"Then can you tell me how on earth you got those two

men inside the sub all by yourself, and one of them not even alive?"

"I don't know, I just did what I had to do, I guess. I got rope burns."

"I noticed."

"The pitching of the sub helped a lot."

"I can imagine. It's a wonder you didn't go right upside down. But didn't the fact that one of the sailors was already dead kind of discourage you from trying, Al?"

"Not really. I promised the man I would go back for his brother. When I think about it now, it's a lot different than it was at the time. I just did what I had to do. That's what happens. A funny kind of energy comes over you."

"Well, that's what they say. I can't imagine it though. Seems to me you're cut out for this seafaring life, Al, more than anybody else I ever heard of. All I can say is, if I'm ever at trouble out at sea, and I sure as heck pray that never happens, I hope it's you coming for me. Good night, Al."

"Good night."

Ziegfried had a way of making me feel ten feet tall.

Chapter Six

∽

WE LEFT SHEBA'S ISLAND on the 1st of July, Canada Day, just after midnight. The sea spread out like an endless field. You'd never know it was the same sea that sank three fishing boats and drowned their fishermen. Sheba and Ziegfried came down and saw us off with hugs, tears and final words of advice, all said many times before. "If you run into any trouble, just turn around and sail back home."

Hollie, Seaweed, and I crowded into the sub. All of the food that could be packed away was fitted tightly into the corners, but the fresh food — bread and cookies, oranges, bananas, tomatoes, grapes, and bags of popcorn — dangled from the ceiling and swung in our way. Most of it would be gone in a week or two but it was nice to begin a journey with lots of fresh food.

We turned the corner of the island and were engulfed by the sea. We had sailed on the open Atlantic before but never across it. Somehow it seemed a lot bigger. Two hundred miles out we would pass over the edge of the continental shelf, where the sea floor suddenly dropped from four hundred feet to two miles. If the sub ever fell to four hundred feet we would be fine, but if we went down a mile or so we'd get flattened like a pancake. Leaving the shelf was a little like going into space in a rocket.

Hollie quickly settled on his spot by the observation window but Seaweed took a sudden fancy to the bicycle seat. It must have been a bird thing — seeking higher ground or something. I didn't mind except that if I wanted to pedal I had to kick him off, and he made a fuss about it.

"Get off, Seaweed, unless you're going to pedal. Then you can stay on as long as you want."

I climbed onto the bike. Ten hours of pedalling would generate about two hours of battery power, which was helpful, although we didn't need it yet; I wanted to pedal for exercise. Seaweed hopped down and took his spot across from Hollie, and stared at him like a vulture. Hollie buried his face in his paws.

"Better get comfortable, Seaweed, we've got a long way to go."

Our first stop would be the Azores, a small group of

islands in the middle of the Atlantic and a possible site of Atlantis. Legend has it Atlantis was either really close to Crete, in the Mediterranean Sea, or somewhere out in the middle of the Atlantic Ocean. It all depends upon how you translate the ancient writings of Plato. It's like a math problem where you have to multiply the answer by either 10 or 1000, depending upon how you understand the question. My gut feeling told me it was closer to Crete. If Atlantis was lying two miles at the bottom of the ocean, nobody was going to find it anyway.

The Azores belong to Portugal and are about twelve hundred nautical miles east of Newfoundland, as the crow flies. In a tossing sea, with wind and current, it might be more like two thousand. Portugal is another seven hundred nautical miles beyond that. Weather permitting, counting time for sleep and unexpected stops, we might expect to reach the Azores in little over a week, assuming we could find them.

Sheba suggested we listen to Portuguese and Spanish radio stations on our way over, so that our spirits would be in the right mood for visiting those countries. I tried that but couldn't tell the difference between Portuguese, Spanish, Italian or Greek. Ziegfried said I'd know it was Spanish if they played a lot of guitar. So I tried that. It was okay for a while, but after a few hours of nothing but guitar music and Spanish voices, Seaweed seemed kind of restless, so I switched back. Hollie didn't seem to care, but Seaweed was happier listening to the sounds of Newfoundland.

Fifteen hours from shore we were approaching the edge of the continental shelf. The sea floor had slipped to five hundred feet and I could feel a deeper drop coming. In our first fifteen hours at sea we hadn't heard a single beep on the radar, which was kind of strange. It gave the impression we were the only vessel out there, and I knew *that* wasn't true. Now, before sailing over waters of extreme depth, where the sub would become like a flea on the surface of a swimming pool, I thought I'd catch some sleep. Hollie and Seaweed could sleep whenever they wanted but I had to stop when I wanted to sleep. I would submerge to two hundred feet, below any passing ships or surface current, turn off all power except the sonar, and climb into my cozy hanging cot. I trusted myself to wake if the sonar beeped, which would only happen if another submarine were passing close by, which was pretty unlikely. What were the chances of two fleas meeting in a swimming pool? Besides, by the Law of the Sea, and for the very first time since we put the sub in the water, we were legal. More than twelve miles from shore, by the United Nations Convention on the Law of the Sea, we had just as much right to be here as anyone else.

My hand was on the switch, ready to dive, when the radar beeped. There was a vessel in the water ten miles away. I waited for a moment. Two beeps appeared on the next sweep. Two vessels. I climbed the portal and scanned the horizon with the binoculars. A line of fog was blowing up from the south; the horizon was too hazy to see clearly. And then it disappeared altogether. Shoot! Now I couldn't see what the vessels were. I didn't want to dive and sleep without knowing what was in the neighbourhood.

Back inside, the two beeps on the radar became three, and then . . . four! Wow! They couldn't have been fishing boats; we were too far from shore. I stared at the radar screen. They were coming slowly towards us. What to do? This was the first time I couldn't race for a cove or settle on the bottom and hide. Five hundred feet was too deep; we might spring a leak. We had two choices: change course and try to get out of the way, or wait and see what was coming. Considering we were legal, I decided to wait.

I cut the engine. We coasted to a drift. I carried Hollie out for a breath of fresh air. Clouds of fog were rolling in faster than the vessels were approaching. They weren't sailing side by side but were about half a mile apart. Maybe they were naval ships. If they were, I would signal a friendly greeting. I could invoke the Law of the Sea Treaty if they questioned our presence.

As the fog thickened to pea soup I couldn't see past the bow. The ships were going to pass unseen. When they were five miles away there were two more beeps on the radar. I climbed inside. Two more vessels were coming from the opposite direction, and they were coming fast! Unbelievably, I watched as the strangest chase scene took place on the radar screen.

The four approaching vessels had obviously become

aware of the two speedy ships because they stopped, turned around one hundred and eighty degrees and cranked up their speed, all four of them together. They were running away! Their pursuers simply ignored us and altered their course to follow the four. And they were *fast!* What was going on? Were the pursuers pirates? That seemed unlikely. In the first place, nobody could see anybody else. Everyone was relying on radar. And yet the pursuing ships must have known about the four ships even before they were within radar range because they had known where to look for them in the first place. They must have had other information, which made me think that maybe the pursuers were the navy or the coastguard.

As much as I was dying to know what was really going on I knew the smartest thing to do was to change course and leave their radar range while we had the chance. And so I did. I turned completely around, headed back the way we had come and made a wide, sweeping arc. I planned to continue our course ten miles south. As we were leaving their radar range, I climbed the portal with the binoculars for one last look. Between pockets of fog on the horizon I thought I caught a glimpse of a red and white ship. The coastguard! Now I probably knew who the pursuers were. But who were they chasing?

That answer came about an hour later when I was again preparing to dive and catch some sleep. The chase jumped back onto the radar screen like a handful of green bugs. First came the four fleeing vessels, travelling much closer together now, and then their pursuers, who had narrowed the gap to less than four miles. Unless I cranked up the engine and took off, both parties would roughly cross our path. I decided to stay, but made ready to dive if necessary.

I cut the engine, climbed the portal with the binoculars and strained to see through the fog. The wind was picking up. It blew holes in the fog here and there. I caught a glimpse of a couple of small ships once or twice, then nothing. The real story was unfolding on the radar screen, but I was hoping to identify the approaching vessels before submerging and letting them pass over us.

It was a strange game of cat and mouse. I kept running inside to check the radar, then climbing the portal and scanning the fog with the binoculars, ready at any moment to dive out of the way.

The fleeing vessels came close, about a mile east of the sub, but not close enough to spot the portal of a small submarine in the fog. They could detect us by radar, of course, but as we weren't even moving, they wouldn't likely consider us a threat. They had bigger things to worry about.

The coastguard entered the screen two and a half miles to the west. We were, in a sense, surrounded. But I was not concerned. The coastguard already knew we were in the area and had shown no interest in us. Whoever they were chasing was obviously a priority. Besides, if any vessel did come too close, we could simply dive, switch to battery power and slip away.

The ships of the coastguard passed within half a mile of us and I never saw them. The fog was too dense. The radar revealed that the fleeing ships had come together in a cluster, close enough to exchange something — crew members perhaps? — and then split up in all directions. They were obviously trying to confuse the coastguard and escape. I wondered what the coastguard would do. Would they split up and chase down two of the four ships, or stay together and chase down one?

The coastguard split up and went after two. It took a while for the radar to reveal what the fog was hiding so well. Two of the fleeing ships turned sharply north and sailed apart. One of the coastguard ships went after one of them; the other stayed behind and continued to follow one of the ships closer to us, which was headed due east. The fourth ship veered south. In a sudden burst of impulsiveness, I decided to chase it.

Chapter Seven

I DIDN'T KNOW WHY I was chasing them except that, if the coastguard wanted them so badly, they must have done something wrong. Besides, I was really curious. But we were all outside the twelve-mile zone. The only rights Canada had in the two hundred mile zone were commercial, and the only commercial interest in the Grand Banks, as far as I knew, was fishing. Was that it? Was the coastguard chasing foreign ships fishing in Canadian waters? But if we were right on the edge of the two hundred mile zone, why would they bother? Couldn't foreign ships simply slip across to the other side of the zone and snub their noses at the coastguard?

I guess not.

She wasn't very fast. With all the changes to the sub, we had no trouble catching her. The coastguard must have caught at least one of her sister ships by now. I could also tell they were not very big, nothing like freighters, because they could turn so easily. And yet, in the heavy fog I couldn't get close enough to see exactly what kind of ship she was, unless . . . I did what submarines were designed to do.

Just when she must have expected us to catch her, I cut the engine, shut the hatch and dove to one hundred feet. I engaged full battery power and continued to track her on sonar. We would have disappeared from her radar instantly, which must have made them wonder what the heck was going on. Perhaps they had some sort of fishing sonar on board, perhaps not, but I doubted they had any idea they were being chased by a submarine.

On battery it took almost an hour to catch and pass her. We went under her like a whale. In the meantime, I watched the sea floor drop from five hundred feet to an unfathomable depth. We had crossed the continental shelf! Cool! But our renegade ship showed no signs of stopping. She was going to get away! Assuming the coastguard had good reason to chase her, I decided to cut her off.

That wasn't hard to do. We sailed about a quarter of a mile in front of her and surfaced. As soon as we broke the surface I turned on our floodlights and coasted to a drift. In the fog she would see our lights before she would be able to make out what sort of vessel we were. Most importantly, we would appear on her radar instantly, directly in front of her! That ought to be enough to convince her to stop. If it wasn't, I was prepared to dive out of the way in a hurry.

Closer and closer she came. I was beginning to feel nervous. I didn't want to get rammed by a ship. Through the periscope I could barely make out her lights. It seemed as though she was slowing down but I couldn't be sure. I kept my hand on the switch, ready to dive. Suddenly, there she was, shrouded in streaks of fog, but lit up like a Christmas tree — a fishing trawler, carrying Spanish colours!

She drifted to a stop. Then I heard the radar beep. Another vessel was coming in fast! In fact, it was already upon us. I raced up the portal and opened the hatch to look. The next thing I knew, I heard machine-gun fire! I jumped back down and got ready to dive, but my curiosity got the better of me and I climbed back up the ladder and peeked over the edge of the hatch. Behind the trawler appeared the red and white hull of a Canadian coastguard ship. Through the binoculars I saw coastguard officers firing machine guns across the bow of the trawler! I couldn't believe it! I watched in amazement as coastguard officers boarded the Spanish ship, arrested the crew and attached a cable from the stern of the coastguard to the bow of the trawler. Were they actually intending to tow the ship all the way back to St. John's?

Yes indeed.

As I stood in the portal and leaned against the hatch, watching the lights of the two ships vanish in the fog, the coastguard blasted her horn. Was that a farewell to us, a salute for our part in the chase? I liked to think so. I waved back. I didn't really understand the significance of what had just happened. That would come later. It had been an exciting chase. Now I needed to sleep.

At two hundred feet we did not have radio. The underwater cable that floated to the surface as an antenna only reached one hundred feet. I didn't mind; we had had enough excitement for one day. Seaweed and Hollie were really good whenever I wanted to sleep. When the sub's interior lights were turned low they went into hibernation mode. I figured that was an animal/bird instinct thing.

There was no surface current at two hundred feet, but there *was* current. It flowed in the opposite direction of the current above, but very slowly. I wasn't really concerned about that. I wasn't worried about sinking either because the sub had an automatic surfacing gauge that we had set at 237.5 feet. If the sub reached that depth unintentionally, the ballast tanks would automatically fill with air and we would surface. There were also two safety ballast balloons attached to the outside of the hull. They contained pressurized cartridges that were designed to explode at four hundred feet, filling two nylon balloons with enough air to raise the sub. It never crossed my mind that the sub might surface for any other reason. I brushed my teeth, stretched, wished the crew a goodnight and climbed into my hanging cot, suspended by bungee cords to compensate for the pitch and toss of the sub. Within minutes I was dead to the world.

I woke eight hours later ... on the surface! I knew we were on the surface because of the movement of the sub, and there was a faint hue coming up through the observation window — light from the sea. I climbed the portal and opened the hatch. It was a clear, sunny day. I looked all around and wondered if I was dreaming. How had we surfaced? Had we drifted down to 237.5 feet and then risen? But why? I would have to make a close inspection of everything and call Ziegfried on the short wave. But first I turned on the radio and listened to the news from St. John's. I wondered if the fishing trawler incident had made the news. It had! And how!

"... Spanish authorities are calling for immediate retaliation. No retaliatory action has been ruled out ... ," said the radio.

Holy smokes! It had become an international story already. As usual, the news-people made it sound like more than it had really been.

"Spain considers Canada's high-seas chase and violent assault on its fishing fleet an act of war," one announcer said.

An act of war! It was just an old beat-up trawler. I was surprised it had crossed the Atlantic without sinking. I sure hoped Canada and Spain wouldn't go to war over it. I tried to reach Ziegfried on the short wave.

"Al! *Como estas?*"

"What?"

"That's Spanish. It means 'how are you?'"

"Oh. Good. Did you hear the news?"

"You bet we did! Did *you* see any Spanish trawlers on your way across the Grand Banks?"

"Uhhh . . . yup."

"Really? Up close?"

"Uhhh . . . sort of."

"Interesting. And everything's working all right?"

"Ummm . . . sort of."

"Sort of? What do you mean, 'sort of?' What's wrong, Al?"

"Nothing really, but the sub rose by itself. I went to sleep at two hundred feet and woke on the surface."

"It surfaced by itself? Ohhhhh . . . that's not good. Listen, Al. You've got to make a thorough inspection of everything right away, okay?"

"I know. I was just about to."

"Good. And then, when you've finished, you've got to run tests. Practise diving, sit in one spot for several hours and watch your depth. See if you sink or rise, okay? This is very important, Al. You must inspect and test everything thoroughly. You know that, right?"

"Yes, I know. Don't worry, I will."

"Maybe you should come back here and we can test it together."

"No. No, it's okay. Maybe I just made a mistake and didn't shut off the air valve properly when I went to sleep."

"Well, check that first, and keep me posted, okay?"

"Okay."

"You promise to keep me posted, right?"

"I promise. I'll start an inspection right away."

"And tests, right?"

"Right."

Yikes! The last thing I wanted to do was return. Ziegfried would run tests all summer long and I wouldn't get back to sea until the fall. After we hung up I began my inspection. Hollie saw me examining things and he immediately joined me, sniffing at every corner with his sharp little nose. Seaweed was up in the sky somewhere. After two hours of close examination I hadn't found anything suspicious at all. When Seaweed returned, I decided to make a test. I shut the hatch, dove to a hundred feet, opened a bag of popcorn and sat in front of the depth gauge.

Seaweed loved popcorn. Hollie didn't care for it much, but if Seaweed was eating, he had to eat too. What they both really liked was catching it. We made a game of it while I stared at the gauge. No change. The sub sat perfectly still for a whole hour.

"Okay, that's it, guys. Let's go."

I decided to continue our journey. I'd call Ziegfried later. He wouldn't be satisfied with my testing, I knew. He was a perfectionist when it came to testing. But I didn't want to hang around in the middle of the ocean doing nothing. And I sure as heck didn't want to return to Newfoundland.

I surfaced, flicked the engine switch and got ready to leave, except . . . there was one little problem: I didn't know where we were. I mean, I didn't know where we were *exactly*. I knew where we were approximately, and I knew that all we had to do was sail east and we'd reach Portugal. But I didn't want to miss the Azores. For that, I had to know with greater certainty where we were. We had obviously drifted with the current after we had surfaced. How far, I didn't know. I had sea charts, of course, but once I lost track of where we were, it was kind of hard to find our exact location. Sea navigation is a lot trickier when you are far from land because of currents and a few other things, such as the fact that *magnetic* north is about eight hundred miles away from *true* north. Basically, you have to take compass readings. Normally that would be impossible on a submarine because of all the metal that interferes with the magnetic pull of the North Pole. But it is possible to compensate for that by placing magnets around the compass in just such a way as to correct for true north. And that's what Ziegfried had done. That was the theory anyway; practise is something else. Even experienced sailors get lost at sea.

After half an hour of taking compass readings, checking the charts carefully and measuring the current, I made my best guess on our position, turned east, cranked up the engine, climbed up on the bike and started to pedal.

I pedalled on and off during the night and listened to the radio. I heated up a frozen pizza, peeled a couple of oranges, made tea and played tug-of-war with a piece of rope. Sea-weed and I teamed up against Hollie, and lost. Hollie was really possessive with his rope. But Seaweed didn't try very hard. He wasn't really interested in closing his beak around anything he couldn't swallow. After a quiet night at sea, dur-ing which we did not encounter a single vessel, we settled at two hundred feet, at a spot I carefully marked on the chart, and went to sleep. In the late afternoon I woke . . . on the surface! And we had drifted.

Chapter Eight

I HAD PROMISED TO keep Ziegfried posted, so I called him
again on the short wave. The weather was good, the reception clear.

"Al! Great! Good to hear from you, buddy. How's the sub
working?"

"Great!"

"Everything's working properly?"

"Yup. Everything's working just right."

"And you made the tests?"

"Yup. The sub never rose or fell an inch."

"And did you find anything wrong?"

"Nope."

"Nothing?"

"Nope."

"So you still don't know why it surfaced by itself?"

"No. I guess it's a mystery."

"Al, submarines don't just surface by themselves. There's got to be something wrong somewhere."

He paused.

"Maybe you'd better bring her back."

"Oh, no, I'm sure everything's all right. It was just a weird thing. I'm sure it won't happen again."

"But if it happens, you'll tell me, right?"

"Uh huh."

"Hmmm . . . I don't like the sound of it, Al, not one little bit."

"It's okay, really. So . . . do you think we're going to war against the Spanish?"

"Holy smokes, I sure hope not! You wouldn't believe the crazy talk here, and the crazy talk there. I'm sure glad you didn't get messed up in that, eh?"

"Yah."

I felt badly for not telling Ziegfried everything, but he would only worry. There would be lots of bumps along the road in my journey. I knew that. I didn't want him to have to worry every single time. After a breakfast of oranges, cookies and dog biscuits with the crew, I took our bearing, made my best guess at the charts, cranked up the engine, climbed onto the bicycle seat and headed east. Seaweed took to the sky. Hollie ran around and around the stationary bike, then wrestled with a piece of rope. I tuned the radio to Spanish guitar.

After a while I climbed the portal to make sure Seaweed was still within sight. Boy, did I get a surprise!

I poked my head out the portal and found myself surrounded by a dozen large, strange-looking geese lined up on the bow and stern, just the way submariners line up during a ceremony. They had obviously flown a long way and were very tired. They tucked their beaks into their feathers and went right to sleep, oblivious to me or to the rather territorial Seaweed, who was making a fuss about it over their heads, to no avail; the geese rested until they were good and ready to leave.

It became common for really tough looking, long-distance seabirds to drop out of the sky and treat the sub like a mini-aircraft carrier. But landing was difficult and sometimes they would miss the hull altogether and hit the sea. Then they would shake the water from their wings and hop up. Seaweed didn't like it but I felt honoured to have them.

On the third night the sky was clear and the stars glittered like diamonds and sapphires. There were so many! If you stared at any black spot long enough, you would eventually see a star. I stood in the portal, mesmerized, with Hollie under my arm and Seaweed on the bow. Once in a while we would hear a splash in the water but wouldn't see anything. Hollie would bark, but I never knew what he was barking at.

After the sun came up, on our fourth day at sea, I dove to two hundred feet, turned the lights low, got cozy and went to sleep. Nine hours later we woke on the surface again, in a tossing sea.

I couldn't believe it! Always the sub was rising to the surface, never sinking, at least not while I was awake. Why was that? I knew I hadn't made tests as thoroughly as Ziegfried would have liked, but I did test a little, and nothing had moved at all. What was going on?

On our fourth night at sea I figured we were roughly halfway to the Azores and probably a bit north. I'd have a better idea when we were closer. The sea was changing now. The small choppy waves had become rising swells. The sun had disappeared in the day. There would be no stars this night. But the biggest indication that bad weather was coming was Seaweed. When we came out for our evening air, he took to the sky but didn't go far. Then, he landed on the stern instead of the bow, and seemed a bit agitated. Very uncharacteristic of him, he came inside earlier than usual. Little did I know what was really on his mind.

It was just a little while later; I was in the engine compartment making a routine inspection when seawater began rushing into the sub! We were diving! Horrified, I raced to the ladder, pulled myself up under the water flooding in, grabbed hold of the hatch, pulled it shut and sealed it. Whew! I was shocked! I was completely soaked. I looked down. Hollie was looking up at me. He was soaked too.

There were several inches of water on the floor and the sump pumps were running full blast trying to remove it. I had a terrible feeling in my stomach. The sub was malfunctioning. We would have to return to Newfoundland. It was too dangerous now.

I felt so disappointed, so terribly disappointed, I could barely contain it. I went to the control panel, slumped down on the seat and dropped my head. I felt like crying. But what would that solve? It was a setback, nothing more. Explorers didn't cry at setbacks; *children* did. The mature thing to do was to recognize that there was a problem and take the proper steps to fix it, even if that meant returning and starting all over again. That's what Ziegfried would have said, and he always knew what he was talking about. If I wanted to survive at sea all by myself, then I had to face the challenges *and* setbacks like an adult. And so, I didn't let myself cry. Instead, I took a deep breath and turned . . . just in time to see Seaweed raise a foot towards the switches. It was him! The little rascal! It was Seaweed all along! I couldn't believe it! I opened my mouth to give him a scolding but caught myself. What was the point in scolding a seagull? Besides, he was a valuable member of the crew. I would just have to watch him around the control panel and cover it with a blanket when I was sleeping. Suddenly I was so happy I wanted to yell. I didn't know if that was very adult-like or not. I did it anyway.

Returning to the surface, I couldn't wait to call Ziegfried

and explain what had happened. But the reception was poor. Ziegfried said there was another storm on the way and that I ought to brace myself. He said to keep a low profile in Spain, too; there was a storm on the political front.

The nice thing about a submarine is that you could simply dive beneath a storm and not even know it was there. But it did make navigation more difficult, and, in truth, I wasn't navigating nearly as well as I thought I would. I would take a bearing, check the sea charts and more or less guess where we were. Then I'd do it an hour later and find that we were too far away from the first reading. We were always moving east, that much I knew for sure. I could always tell by the sun and stars, although the sun and stars were covered now and we only had the compass. And the worse the weather became, the poorer the compass reading was.

There wasn't much danger to the sub in a storm, but getting tossed around on the surface could get pretty uncomfortable and seasickness was hard to avoid. So, we would submerge. Beneath the surface we had twenty hours of battery power when the batteries were fully charged, and I could pedal. All together we could sail for about twenty-two hours submerged, which might be enough to sail out of the storm if it were blowing in the opposite direction. If it were blowing in the same direction it was better to stay where we were and let it pass, although twenty-two hours submerged was kind of hard on the crew. We had to surface from time to time anyway to fill the air compressors. We needed a constant supply of compressed air for diving, surfacing and breathing. I kept a close eye on the air gauges as a matter of habit. That's what was difficult about a storm — the inconvenience. On the sea, they started earlier and lasted longer. Having said that, I had to admit that storms at sea were pretty exciting. You never knew *what* might be coming your way . . .

Chapter Nine

I THOUGHT I WAS dreaming. The sonar was blinking away, as if there were a giant object closing in on us. I was caught in that place between sleep and waking, where you're not really sure if it's a dream or not. I opened my eyes. The sonar *was* blinking! I jumped to my feet and ran to the screen. There *was* a giant object outside! We were in the middle of the Atlantic Ocean, two hundred feet below the surface and there was a gigantic object immediately outside. I felt panic.

There was a tapping sound, like metal against glass. I turned my head. The tapping was coming from the observation window. I moved slowly towards the window as if I were floating through a nightmare. Flicking on the lights, I saw a face in the window staring up at me. He was inside a diving suit, his face pressed against the window. He gave me a thumbs-up with a questioning look. Was I all right? I gave a thumbs-up back, smiled awkwardly, then made the gesture for sleeping. I was okay; I had just been sleeping. He nodded, gave a thumbs-up again and saluted goodbye. I lifted the blanket off the control panel and flipped the switch to surface. As we rose, I watched the enormous object below slowly begin to move away. The sound of her motor was muffled and eerie, and the vibration made my teeth chatter. A nuclear-powered submarine — American, Russian, British, or French — I didn't know which, but they had been incredibly friendly, stopping to check and see if I was all right. I put the kettle on for tea, fed the crew some dog biscuits and sat down to clear my head. Ziegfried had once said, "Don't think you'll be the only submarine in the sea." And how!

The storm had moved on, although the sea still rolled in large swells. At least it was sailable. Seaweed was happy to get into the sky again, and followed us closely, gliding in the wind like a kite. Hollie was anxious to stand in the portal with me and lean into the breeze, sniffing it for rabbits.

"I don't think there are any rabbits here, Hollie."

He didn't care; he sniffed for them anyway. We were heading east; I had the sun behind the clouds to verify that. I would do my best to determine where we were exactly, but first needed time to get over the shock of the sudden wakening and unexpected company. Nuclear submarines patrolled the seas like it was nobody's business. They could show up anywhere at anytime. But you would hardly expect one to stop and check out a tiny sub like mine, unless maybe there was a special camaraderie amongst submariners, as there was amongst sailors. Now the thought of that made me feel special.

For two more nights we sailed without event, sleeping in the days without visitors or interruption. But I was beginning to worry that we had passed the Azores. I scanned the charts and took lots of compass readings but could never say with certainty where we were. I never thought of it as being lost, only that we didn't know exactly where we were, which wasn't the same thing. Then, one night while watching the stars and noticing that sometimes at sea you would find stars very close to the horizon, I saw the brightest star sitting right *on* the horizon. Hollie saw it too. And it was blinking! Then I realized it wasn't a star at all, it was a lighthouse! We had found the Azores! Yes!

A few hours later we were sitting in the water just a quarter of a mile from the northern cliffs of Corvo, the smallest and most northwesterly island of the Azores. The powerful lighthouse was lighting up Hollie's eager, whiskered face every few seconds or so. Otherwise, we were in total darkness. Standing in the portal I heard the sonar beep. The sonar? But no radar? That was kind of strange. I went inside. According to the sonar, three vessels roughly our size were coming in quickly to meet us. Submarines? Did they patrol their island with mini-submarines? I couldn't believe it.

I wondered if we should try to escape. What if they took the sub away from us? A sudden worry raced through my head: how would I ever get Seaweed home? Hollie would be allowed on a plane, no doubt, but would they let me travel with a seagull? Before I could decide what to do, there were two more beeps on the sonar. Two more mini-subs? Now we were surrounded!

I climbed the portal with Hollie still in my arms and he was barking the way he barked at rabbits. We heard a loud splash. Could they surface so quickly? There was another splash, so close that it sprayed us. By now we ought to have heard them on the radar but there was nothing. What kind of submarines were these?

In the moonlight I caught a glimpse of the outline of one as it rose out of the water and dove again, slapping its tail on the way down. Hollie barked ferociously after it. I laughed. These weren't submarines; these were whales!

We leaned against the portal and listened to the whales until the sky turned a dark blue and an orange line appeared in the east. The whales became visible. Hollie's bark had dwindled to a menacing growl, like a stuffed toy with a tiny motor vibrating in its belly. I had never seen whales up close before, except once, when a dead one drifted in with the tide. These whales were beautiful and playful. They really seemed to be playing. I could have watched them all day.

The sky brightened and the cliffs of Corvo glistened with light when the sun came over the horizon. I raised the binoculars to take a closer look at the cliffs and saw a man climbing down on steps cut into the rock. He was making his way quickly and waving his arms frantically. He was waving at us! He must have spotted us from the lighthouse. He seemed awfully anxious for us to come to shore. I went inside and grabbed the bag of flags. Sheba had fashioned the Portuguese, Spanish, French, Italian, and Greek flags out of material from old dresses. The colours were not exact and the designs not perfect, but they looked pretty good from a distance. It was a courtesy to fly the flag of the country in whose waters you were sailing, as well as your own flag so they knew where you were from. I hooked the Canadian and Portuguese flags to the portal. The wind unfurled them and held them aloft. I steered towards the cliff and came in cautiously, keeping an eye on the sea floor with the sonar. It was just as steep beneath the surface as it was above. Could Atlantis be down there?

I held my passport in my pocket, ready to present it as soon as it was demanded. We came within a hundred feet of the cliff but I could see no place to tie up. I waved to the man and he waved back excitedly. I pulled out my passport. He strained to see it, then, guessing what it was, frowned impatiently and gestured for me to put it away. I put it back in my pocket. He made the gesture of eating and pointed up to the lighthouse. I nodded and went searching for a place to moor the sub.

His name was Arturo. He was the lighthouse keeper. He was short and stocky and had wavy black hair and a friendly face. His wife's name was Anna. She was very beautiful and exceptionally friendly. They welcomed me as if I were the first person ever to visit them. Anna made a huge fuss over Hollie right away and I wondered if he was the first dog she had ever seen. Not at all. The way she picked him up and looked into his eyes showed she was a serious dog-lover. They had a daughter too — Nicola. Nicola was about my age, and was kind of . . . well, gothic. She had piercings on her earlobes, her eyebrows, nose and bottom lip. She had blue and green streaks in her hair and black fingernail polish. She kept staring at me as if I had come from the moon. She was easily the most beautiful girl I had ever seen, and I had a hard time not staring at her.

When we entered the house, which was attached to the lighthouse, I saw that the table had already been set for breakfast, with a plate set for me. I had barely said more than a few words when they started pushing food in front of me. Anna also prepared a plate for Hollie, with whom she had fallen in love. She set his plate on the table, too, but I insisted he eat on the floor. I didn't want him to get spoiled or develop bad habits, such as eating off tables. Hollie looked up at me as if to say, "You never treat me like this." I looked back sternly. "Don't get used to it."

Arturo was the only one who spoke English, and it was kind of hard for me to understand. He said he had once been a sailor and had visited Canada. He said that St. John's had the friendliest pubs in the world. Anna and Nicola just smiled a lot and poured affection on Hollie, who sucked it up like a sponge. I wondered if I was going to have a hard time getting him to leave when it was time to go.

I asked Arturo if there was a place on the island where I should present my passport but he said, no, forget about it. On his island nobody cared. If I went to any of the bigger islands, then, yes, it might be a problem. Then he began to tell me how he loved to watch whales early in the morning and how amazed he was to discover that one of the whales was really a submarine. Anna wanted to know — did I really sail across the Atlantic? I nodded. All alone? Yes, well . . . I pointed to Hollie. She put her hands over her heart. Then I made the gesture of a squawking bird, but, try as I might, I could not get them to understand that the other member of the crew was a seagull.

After breakfast Arturo asked me if I would like to see the light. I said I would love to. I reached for Hollie but Anna had him cradled in her lap and pleaded with me to leave him behind. Okay, I thought. "Be good, Hollie," I said. But he ignored me.

I followed Arturo up the spiralling staircase of the lighthouse tower. The steps went up and up and up! It was hard to believe that the tiny light I had seen from so far away was sitting on top of such a tall tower. I was out of breath by the time we reached the top but Arturo wasn't even breathing hard. Being a lighthouse keeper was really good for your health!

When we came out at the top we entered a room with windows all around. The view was amazing. I could see the whole of the island and far out to sea in all directions. Arturo slapped the giant prism that reflected the light and told me proudly that they didn't make lights like this anymore. I asked him if he liked being a lighthouse keeper. He took a deep breath and said it was the best job in the world. Look how far you can see on a clear day, he said, and pointed out to sea. I looked. Then he pointed in another direction and told me to look there. So I did. After fifteen minutes or so I thought we might go back down to the house but Arturo was content to stay where he was. I leaned against the window and stared down to where the sub was moored, though I couldn't see it. I did see a few seagulls but couldn't tell if Seaweed was one of them. I wondered, would Portuguese seagulls squawk in Portuguese?

After half an hour I had had enough of staring at the ocean from such a height. It was a beautiful view, sure enough, but it was pretty much all the same. Yet Arturo never seemed to tire of it. "Look over there," he said. And I looked, but didn't see anything different. After an hour I was starting to think that being a lighthouse keeper was maybe the most boring job in the world.

Nicola rescued me. She had climbed the steps and appeared suddenly without a sound. She looked like an angel in a gothic costume. She said a few words quietly to Arturo. He responded with strong, forceful words, as if he were reprimanding her, then broke into a big smile and kissed her on the forehead. Nicola surprised me by taking me by the hand and leading me down the steps. After half a dozen steps or so, I pulled my hand free. I wasn't going to walk all the way down the lighthouse steps with my hand in a girl's.

When we came into the house, Anna was sitting on a sofa with Hollie, brushing his short, bristly hair lovingly. Hollie continued to ignore me. He was already spoiled. Nicola led me outside and onto the path towards the cliff. I followed obediently. From her gestures I gathered that she wanted to see my submarine. That meant another steep climb all the way down and back up the cliff. Holy smokes! But I went obediently.

I didn't know if Nicola could swim or not and so I was very careful leading her to the sub. I had moored it between two sections of rock and tied it in three places to keep it from scraping. This time I took her hand firmly as we climbed from the rock to the sub, jumping onto the hull. She didn't seem the least bit afraid. It was pretty weird to bring a girl to my sub.

I opened the hatch and gestured for her to climb inside, which she did like an expert. I followed her in and threw the light switches and turned on the radio. Her face broke into a big smile. She looked around. She ran her fingers over the control panel, which made me a little nervous. I got ready to act in case she flipped any switches. But she didn't. She moved into the bow and knelt down and looked down through the observation window and exclaimed, "Oh!" Then said something in Portuguese.

Nicola explored the whole sub, touching everything. She gripped my swinging cot and swung it around and laughed. She opened my little fridge and freezer and laughed again. She stooped and tried to read the labels on my canned food and touched the remaining hanging tags of not-so-fresh food. I wondered if she found it kind of smelly. I always had fresh air, but a submarine had its own way of smelling after you had been to sea for a while, especially if you were travelling with a dog and seagull. Speaking of which, Seaweed suddenly dropped inside the portal and Nicola jumped back in alarm.

"It's okay, it's okay," I said. "This is Seaweed. He is part of the crew. His . . . name . . . is . . . Sea . . . weed."

"Zeeeee . . . vvvvid," she said.

"Yes."

I liked the way she said it. Seaweed couldn't have cared less. He was wondering what there was to eat. I handed a couple of dog biscuits to Nicola and gestured for her to feed him. She bent down and carefully reached them out. Seaweed twisted his head sideways and looked at her impatiently.

"No, you have to throw them," I said. "He won't take them from your hand."

"*Que?*" she said.

I made the gesture for tossing. She stood up quickly and tossed a biscuit. It went wide but Seaweed caught it easily. Nicola laughed. She threw another, making it harder to catch, but Seaweed caught it. She looked for another; she was delighted.

"I don't want to overfeed him," I said, even though I knew you couldn't overfeed a seagull. I gave her two more biscuits. She threw them wide again and Seaweed caught them easily, but I didn't think he was in the mood for playing. I could hear other seagulls outside. When I didn't give her any more, Seaweed got the message and bolted up the ladder. Nicola watched him climb and burst out laughing. Her laughter was so pleasant; I was thinking how nice it would be to have more of her company. I had no idea just how eagerly she was thinking the same thing.

Chapter Ten

꙳

I SHOULD HAVE been sleeping, it was past my bedtime, but I couldn't communicate that to my hosts who were being so kind to me. In the middle of morning Anna sent Nicola and me up the steps of the lighthouse with a cup of coffee and a plate of cookies for Arturo. My legs were beginning to get sore as I lagged behind Nicola on the way up. When we entered the room at the top, Arturo made a big fuss over us, as if he hadn't seen us for months. He kissed Nicola on the forehead again, took me over to the window and pointed distantly towards the horizon. I strained my eyes to see, but all I could see was water and sky. I was pretty sure that's all that was there, though he was acting as if it were something extraordinary. On the way down the steps my legs hurt even more than going up. When we got to the bottom and entered the house, Hollie was wearing a hat!

I had grown so sleepy all I wanted to do was return to the sub, submerge and crawl into my cozy bed. Instead, I ended up spending the afternoon with Nicola. Her parents seemed delighted she had company. We played cards, worked on an enormous jigsaw puzzle of a picture of horses, and she told me the names of many things in Portuguese. And though I was too tired to concentrate, and couldn't remember a single word, I loved sitting across from her anyway and just watching her. If there *were* mermaids, as Sheba firmly believed, I was convinced they would look like Nicola, except maybe without the piercings.

At supper, Arturo asked me where I was going next. I said I was looking for Atlantis. Had they ever heard of Atlantis being located in the Azores? Oh, yes, Arturo said. They had? Yes. Wow! That's great! Did he have any idea where? Of course, he said. Would he show me? Of course, as soon as we finished supper.

And so, with a belly full of stew, bread and cheese, I followed Arturo up the lighthouse steps one more time, though I fell far behind. My legs were terribly sore and I was so sleepy I was dizzy. Finally, I reached the top and entered the room where Arturo was anxiously waiting to show me where Atlantis was. I caught my breath. Where? There. He pointed out the window. I looked. He was pointing out to sea. What, way out there? Yes, he said. And there! He pointed in another direction. Really? Atlantis? Yes, he said. And there! He pointed somewhere else. "There!" he said emphatically. Then he opened his arms wide and swung around in a circle. "There!" he said. "Atlantic!" I shut my eyes. Oh. He thought I meant the ocean.

Back downstairs I thanked everyone for their wonderful hospitality. They begged me to stay but I explained that I had far to go and not much time. Anna asked: could I just leave Hollie? I said I was very sorry but Hollie was part of the crew. Nicola looked upset. She gave me a polite kiss on the cheek then disappeared. I stumbled back to the sub as it was getting dark. Hollie followed me but kept looking around, and Anna followed him across the field and even down the cliff a few steps. I was too tired to explain anything to Hollie; I just said, "Hollie! Come!" in my firmest tone. And he obeyed. But he whined and looked like somebody leaving a party just when it was becoming fun.

It wasn't easy getting down the cliff with sore legs. It was almost dark, the time we would normally be waking. I climbed onto the sub only to discover that in my distracted state earlier I had left the hatch open. How strange! I had never done that before. Oh, well, I climbed in, shut the hatch, dove to fifty feet, shut the lights and dropped onto my bed. I fell asleep instantly.

It was early morning when I woke. Now my sleep was backwards. I surfaced and opened the hatch. Seaweed appeared immediately. He had an amazing way of keeping track of the sub submerged. I fed the crew, made a cup of tea and headed out to sea. An hour later I heard a strange noise in the stern. Turning, I was shocked to discover we had a stowaway!

It was Nicola. She must have climbed in before me and was hiding in the stern all night long, the poor thing. She smiled with an awkward look on her face, and then said something excitedly in Portuguese. With pleading gestures she communicated that she wanted to stay. She wanted to join the crew!

I knew that wasn't a good idea. And it should have been an easy decision to turn around and take her back home. But it wasn't. In the first place, she was very, very persistent. Even though we didn't speak the same language I could understand a lot of what she was saying just by the look on her face. Like me, she didn't want to stay where she was raised and live the life that her parents were offering her. She wanted to get out into the world and explore. I could understand that. We were the same age. We would probably experience a lot of things in the same way, and that would be fun. It would be fun teaching her how to sail the submarine, and how to dive, and how to do lots of things. And she would be great company. And she was so pretty.

It was one time that I honestly didn't want to ask myself what Ziegfried would do, because I already knew. One part of me just wanted to have fun and didn't want to worry about what was the "right" thing to do, or what other people were going to think. It didn't help that Arturo and Anna probably already thought it was my idea. Or maybe they even thought that I had kidnapped her! Sheba had told me that the Trojan War was started because Paris had kidnapped Helen from Greece, and that the Greeks went to war to get her back. But, in fact, nobody really knew if Helen had actually been kidnapped or had gone of her own free will because she had fallen in love with Paris. Yikes! If I did turn around, not only would I have to deal with Nicola's deep disappointment, but her father's anger too. I wasn't looking forward to either.

But I owed it to Ziegfried to try to think of what he would say. I remembered watching my grandfather's shotgun slip out of his hands and disappear into the water. That must not have been easy for him to do, to go against my grandfather's wishes for me, and yet he did it. He did what he believed was the right thing to do. My grandfather was being caring in the best way he knew how, too. They just showed it in different ways. Both put a lot of faith in me. Well, I couldn't betray that faith by acting in such an irresponsible way. That decided it!

Nicola didn't just pout when I turned the sub around, she cried all the way in, and it took a whole hour! It was the worst thing I ever had to listen to. She cried and wailed and pleaded like a little girl. At one point she even lay on the floor and kicked her arms and legs up in the air. I tried turning on the radio but she just cried louder. Well, that certainly convinced me my decision was right — if this was how she dealt with such a setback, then she clearly wasn't ready to leave home and go to sea.

Arturo was standing on the rock when I pulled up to moor the sub. I waved to him and tried to explain what had happened, but he didn't seem angry with me at all. He *was* angry with Nicola. She stopped crying when she saw him. She just rolled her eyes, sighed loudly and dropped her head. I watched them climb the cliff, while he gave her an earful. Then I returned to the sub and headed out to sea. I took a deep breath and shrugged. I had heard of lonely lighthouse keepers before, but a whole family?

Arturo had advised that I avoid Sao Miguel, the biggest island with the largest population. If I were seen around there, he said, the authorities would definitely want to stamp my passport and insist that I stay around for at least a few days while they examined my submarine. I shouldn't have too much trouble with Graciosa, though, a smaller island with just five thousand people or so. I decided not to risk it. I was not so anxious to step onto land that I'd take the chance of being delayed. But I did sail close enough to Graciosa to take a peek at the island through the binoculars.

It was completely different from Corvo. It had a mountain in the center but was low-lying on the north side and appeared to have a decent harbour. I picked up several fast vessels on radar, likely recreational boaters enjoying the warm summer afternoon. Sure enough, through the binoculars I caught a glimpse of some water-skiers and jet-skiers. We went by about a mile out with our flags down so as not to draw attention. We were on the surface, that was all the Law of the Sea required of foreign submarines within the twelve-mile zone. It was a lovely, sleepy summer's afternoon as we passed the beautiful island. Hollie seemed to have forgotten the lady of the lighthouse already and was enjoying the warm breeze sweeping over the portal. Everything was just about perfect, until . . . I started to get that premonition feeling.

"It must be my imagination, Hollie. What do you think?"

Hollie wasn't sure. He bit his lip and looked up in the sky at Seaweed doing his kite thing. From the portal I could hear the radar beeping inside. What was it that was bugging me?

I climbed down the ladder and took a look at the screen. In one corner of the bay were three motorboats that showed up as three lights on the radar. Those were the water-skiers. They were taking turns running up a platform; I could see them with the binoculars. On the other side of the bay were two jet-skis crisscrossing the harbour like jousting knights. That looked like a lot of fun. But . . . the radar showed *three* vessels. I climbed the portal and gazed through the binoculars. There were definitely just two jet-skiers. Hmmm, that was strange. I went back inside. There were three beeps on the radar, though only two were moving. Those were the jet-skiers. What was sitting in the water between them?

I went back outside. It was such a gorgeous day. We were

passing them now. If any of the boaters and skiers looked out very carefully they might have seen us sailing past, but everyone was too busy having fun to stare out to sea. I scratched my head. Whatever was sitting in the water between the jet-skiers, surely they must have known what it was? But there was that feeling again. And then, I remembered what Sheba had said . . . "trust those feelings." Oh boy.

"What do we do, Hollie, move on . . . or investigate? Hmmm?"

Actually, I knew what Hollie would think. He was an investigating kind of dog.

"Okay . . . we'll move a little closer."

So, I shut the hatch, submerged to periscope level and quietly entered the bay. I knew we were not supposed to submerge inside the twelve-mile zone but I was only planning to take a quick peek, then leave. Whatever was sitting in the water between the jet-skiers must have been made of metal because it showed up on radar. What if they didn't know it was there and ran into it? They could get killed!

Back and forth the jet-skiers raced towards each other, crossed paths, then swung out to the far sides of their figure eight. They reached the corners of their loop at about the same time, paused to wave to each other, then raced together again. They certainly looked like knights on horseback without the long spears. I noticed the submerged object between them had shifted a little bit. It must have been drifting in with the tide. What *was* it?

Through the periscope there was no way I could tell what it was. And so, at quarter of a mile away I surfaced. I opened the hatch and quickly raised our flags. Now we were clearly visible to the boaters and anyone on shore who might care to look our way. But nobody stopped doing what they were doing; everyone was having such a good time.

Slowly, cautiously, we came closer. I stood up on top of the portal and stared hard with the binoculars. Now I could definitely see something in the water. It was floating just beneath the surface and creating a round bald space in the waves. A little closer . . . I thought I saw something sticking up. A little closer still . . . yes, there was definitely something sticking up. There were several sharp things sticking up. Closer still . . . they appeared to be spikes, sharp spikes sticking up from a big, black, round . . . oh, my gosh! I froze! It was a sea mine! It was a World War II sea mine! The jet-skiers were in terrible danger! So was everyone on the beach! So were we!

Chapter Eleven

⁓

SEA MINES WERE ghosts from the war. They were designed to blow up when they were struck by the hull of a ship and send the crew to a watery grave. But sometimes they blew up from the vibration of a ship's engine, or even when they merely detected an electrical current different from their own. They were dropped into the sea by the thousands during the war. Afterwards, special ships called minesweepers went around and cleaned them up. But they couldn't possibly find them all because many had drifted so far away. Sometimes they drifted for fifty years or more and floated to strange places, such as up rivers with the tide, and buried themselves in mud and sewage, waiting for someone to find them and set them off. Many years later they were still kill-ing the grandchildren of the soldiers who had been fighting when the mines were first dropped in the sea! Talk about a sinister weapon!

The jet-skiers saw the sub and stopped jousting. They stood up on their motored mounts and stared at me as I drew closer to the mine. My plan was to keep the area around the mine clear until the authorities came out to take care of it. Then I would explain exactly what had happened. I would have tried to reach them by short wave but I couldn't speak Portuguese.

So I waited and waited, but nobody came. The jet-skiers waited too, and drifted closer. They could see me staring at something, but I think they were more afraid of the sub than some unknown object in the water. I waved to them and pointed to the mine but they didn't understand. Then I realized, they were even younger than me. They were just kids!

The mine was drifting in. Soon it would be in danger of striking a rock on the floor of the bay. There were swimmers on the beach and people lying on towels watching us, but nobody coming out. I couldn't wait any longer. I went inside and tied my longest ropes together and made a lasso. I shut the engine and moved closer on battery power to about two hundred feet from the mine, then tied one end of the rope to the hatch and threw the rest over my shoulder and jumped into the water. I swam over and carefully tossed the rope over the mine. It took five tries, and I shut my eyes every time, as if *that* was going to help. Then I swam back to the sub. My plan was to pull the mine out to deeper water and figure out what to do with it later. The jet-skiers finally seemed to understand what was going on because they stopped inching closer, spun around suddenly and bolted away.

As soon as I climbed into the sub, flipped the engine switch and pulled the rope taut . . . the mine blew up! It made a terrible blast, like a sharp crack of thunder. I climbed the portal. Rain was falling down in the sunshine. A large wave formed and was rushing outward. It hit the sub and splashed me in the face. I grabbed the binoculars and took a quick scan. I didn't think anyone had been hurt. People were gathered on the beach and pointing excitedly towards us. There was no doubt in my mind what to do next . . . get the heck out of there! I jumped back inside, dove to periscope depth and headed straight out to sea. I would have dived deeper but wanted Seaweed to be able to track us. I wanted to get out of the twelve-mile zone before somebody caught us. I would feel a lot more comfortable explaining the situation in international waters.

From two miles out I watched on radar a handful of small boats collect in the bay, but no one came after us. I surfaced, waved a slice of bread in the air and waited for Seaweed. He didn't show up. Shoot! That was strange. He was so good at keeping us in sight. Something must have distracted him.

Then, I had a terrible thought: where was Seaweed when the mine exploded?

We had to go back.

We couldn't come in on the surface now, not after having fled. If they believed we had caused the explosion, then saw us racing back in, they might think we were coming to do it again. I sat for a moment and tried to think. What would I do if I were protecting a harbour and knew there was a foreign submarine in the area? That was easy, I'd do the same thing the Canadian coastguard and navy would do, I'd bring in airplanes and helicopters. I'd drop sensitive listening devices into the water and set up a radar net offshore with half a dozen ships. That's what I would do, and so that's what I decided to prepare for.

I didn't know how much time we had to get inside the bay and hide, and hiding was definitely what we had to do. If they did bring aircraft, they'd spot us so easily it wasn't funny, unless we were submerged beneath something. And the only thing we could submerge beneath was a boat.

It didn't take long to get back into the bay. We were sailing on battery at periscope depth. There were already more boaters in the bay. Probably the water-skiers had come over for a look. There were also some stationary vessels closer to shore. Moored sailboats? I scanned with the periscope. Yes, there were a handful of sailboats a couple of hundred meters off the beach. To the right was a small pier raised on wooden stilts. I wondered how deep it was beneath the pier.

I submerged completely and came in just above the bay floor. Past experience taught me that if Seaweed saw the periscope, there was a good chance he'd be riding on top of it. So much for invisibility.

With sonar I guided the sub to a slow stop directly beneath the sailboat closest to the pier, then shut off the batteries and turned off the sonar. Now we could not know what was going on above, but at least we were undetectable. I would wait until the middle of night, then carefully surface to periscope depth and take a peek. In the meantime I figured Hollie and I could get some sleep, although it was hard to sleep wondering if Seaweed was okay.

It was three-thirty when I let enough air into the ballast tanks to rise to periscope level. I did it gently, trying to make as little sound as possible. I didn't turn on the sonar, because if they had put any kind of listening devices into the bay they would immediately pick up our sonar waves and know we were there. I climbed onto the bike and pedalled just enough to move the sub out from underneath the sailboat. I didn't want to bump into it coming up.

As soon as the periscope broke the surface I spun it around searching for lights. There were boats in the bay still, and boats offshore, though nothing was moving. Was it a radar net? Probably. I would deal with that later. I was more concerned with finding Seaweed first. For that, I had to surface.

I brought the sub up so that the portal was just a foot

above the surface but the bow and stern were still submerged. In the darkness, right next to the sailboat, I didn't think anyone would see us. As quietly as possible I opened the hatch and stuck my head out. Would Seaweed be waiting there, as he so often was? No, he wasn't. But there was a man in the sailboat, and he was as surprised as heck to see *me*.

"Thundering tarnation! What the . . . who are *you*?"

I was at least relieved to hear that he spoke English. He sounded like maybe he was from England.

"My name is Alfred. I'm from Canada."

"Canada? *Canada*? But . . . but you're the one they're out looking for. You're the one who blew up the bay."

"I didn't blow up the bay, I was trying to remove a dangerous mine and it blew up."

"A sea mine?"

"Yah!"

"Really?"

"How else could there have been such an explosion?"

"I don't know . . . because you are in a submarine, going around blowing up things. What are you doing in a submarine in the first place?"

"Exploring."

"You're exploring in a submarine?"

"Yes."

"And you sailed here all the way from Canada?"

"Yes."

He folded his arms together, nodded his head up and down

and looked at me as if he were trying to make up his mind.

"How old are you?"

"Fifteen."

"You are, aren't you?"

"Yes."

For a minute, neither of us knew what to say. I was guessing he was about sixty.

"Were they looking for me with helicopters today?"

"Well, I guess so! Helicopters, airplanes, boats and scooters."

"Scooters?"

"Jet-skis."

"Oh. I would have escaped already but I had to come back for a crew member."

"A crew member? I thought you were all by yourself. Your submarine looks pretty small for a crew."

"It's a seagull."

"Now you're putting me on."

"No, it's true. His name is Seaweed."

"Well, I don't know what to think, but you'd better come up for a drink there, young Alfred. What do you say?"

"Sure."

Chapter Twelve

c❀

HIS NAME WAS REGGIE. He was from Australia. He lived in his sailboat and sailed it around and around the world. But it took him a very long time. His last trip around the world took nine years. The one before that took twelve. He was married six times — to four different women! He said he'd explain that one after he had a drink. He used to be a wine dealer in Australia, but one day he impulsively sold his business and his house, bought his sailboat and never looked back. The Azores, he said, was one of his favourite places to "dry out." I didn't know if he meant dry out from the sea or dry out from drinking.

After I carried Hollie up the portal, shut the hatch and

climbed onto the sailboat, Reggie brought out a rope and tire and we tied our vessels together so that the sub's portal was tucked in tightly beneath the bow of the sailboat, with the tire in between to prevent chafing. The water in the bay was calm.

"Yah, they took a close look at the bay with their helicopters and chased you pretty far out to sea. They're probably still chasing you."

"I think they've set up a radar net," I said, and pointed out at the ships on the horizon.

Reggie strained to see.

"Is *that* what they're doing out there? Well, you're a clever bugger, aren't you? I get the feeling you've been through something like this before."

"I have."

He grinned.

"Here they are . . . scanning the water for a toothpick in a haystack, and there you are hiding right beneath my boat like nobody's business. I'd say that calls for a drink!"

He disappeared into the cabin and returned with a bottle of wine and two glasses. He wiped the glasses with his shirt, filled them with wine and handed one to me. I had never had wine before but figured I'd just sip it to be friendly. Reggie raised his glass in the air.

"Well, here's to the most impromptu meeting I've ever had on the water, and to a brand new friendship!"

We clinked glasses and I took a tiny sip. It tasted like very strong bitter tea without sugar or milk. Why would anyone drink that? Reggie emptied half of his glass in one go.

"So, now, you're missing your crew. They've jumped ship, have they? Well, I have a feeling I know where that seagull of yours is."

"Really? You do?"

"Yes, I think I do."

"How? Where?"

"You see that hill over there?"

He pointed to the lights of a little village about a mile away.

"Yes?"

"Well, on the other side of it there is an open dump."

"Okay . . . so?"

"Well, at the dump there are a couple of hundred seagulls. I reckon your first mate has gotten himself mixed up in a big seagull party and forgot all about his ship leaving port. Wouldn't be the first time a sailor got left behind."

I wondered if he was right. Seaweed certainly liked to mingle with other seagulls whenever we came to shore but had never stayed behind before. The thought of him hanging around a dump didn't impress me very much.

"Do you think you could tell me how to get there so I can see if he's there?"

"I'll do better than that, Captain. I'll take you there myself."

So, Reggie, Hollie, and I climbed into a rubber dinghy and rowed to shore. It was still dark. The sun would be up in an hour. I was worried the authorities might spot me and wonder who I was, but Reggie shrugged it off.

"Nah, don't worry about that. Nobody will be out of bed for hours, and they wouldn't care anyway."

Hollie was delighted to be onshore once again and ran around at top speed. I walked beside Reggie at a snail's pace. Everything about his movements was slow and easy-going. In his unbuttoned shirt, wrinkled skin and worn-out sandals, he had the look of someone who had been on vacation for so long he didn't know how to do anything else. I would have liked to walk faster but he kept reassuring me that it wasn't far and that I needn't worry about the villagers waking up and discovering me. "For all they know," he said, "you're just another bozo on the bus."

We passed the village and climbed the hill. The horizon had turned blue behind us and we were beginning to hear birds. Hollie settled into a trot beside us and kept his nose close to the ground, attentive to every sound and smell. Once in a while I picked up the scent of something foul, as if we were approaching a dead carcass or something. The higher we went, the more frequent those whiffs of bad air became. Hollie seemed to be very interested in them. When we reached the summit, turned to the left and went around a bluff, a powerful rancid smell hit us. Just as Reggie had said, the beautiful hill concealed an open-pit dump, which looked like a small volcanic crater filled with garbage. On the far side, halfway around the rim, was a large flock of seagulls, not yet awakened to the day. The first rays of sun were about to break from the edge of the sea.

Staring at a couple of hundred sleeping seagulls, I had no idea how to find Seaweed. Then, something occurred to me.

"Hollie?"

He looked up eagerly.

"Go find Seaweed!"

I didn't even have to say it twice. Hollie took off as if it were the most important mission of his life.

"Well, look at that!"

Reggie was impressed. I was proud. Hollie ran around the circumference of the dump, dodging piles of garbage here and there and occasionally jumping over things. As he approached one end of the flock, the birds began to unsettle. Two or three hopped into the air, and then — with a sound like a rushing wind — the whole flock rose. They lifted off the ground like a carpet, and their morning cries pierced the air like sirens. Hollie ran beneath them, barking his little head off. He was in his glory.

I waited for a few minutes, while the seagulls spread out in the sky and began to wind upwards in a spiral. Some headed towards the sea, many just settled back on the ground, and one flew directly towards us.

"Seaweed! You rascal!"

I took a handful of dog biscuits from my pocket, tossed one towards him and one towards Hollie, who was racing back. That was not a good idea! Suddenly, hundreds of seagulls descended upon us and I realized my mistake — you didn't feed one seagull at a dump! We turned on our heels in a hurry and headed back towards the village.

I was anxious to return to the sub before we were spotted, but Reggie insisted we stop by a certain bakery that would just be opening.

"You can't beat Portuguese bakeries," he said, "and the smell of freshly baked bread in the morning!"

He was right. In all my life I never smelled anything so wonderful. We stepped into the bakery in the front of an old house. Loaves of bread and dozens of pastries were stacked on shelves like bundles of gold. I wanted to eat everything! But I didn't have any Portuguese money. No worries, Reggie said. He bought two loaves of bread and a bag of pastries. The baker already knew Reggie and insisted we take extra pastries for free. When Reggie introduced me, the baker shook my hand and I noticed that his hands smelled good too.

We stuffed our faces on the way back to the boat, then Hollie and I returned to the sub to sleep. Seaweed stayed on the boat with Reggie. They had taken a shine to each other, which was unusual for Seaweed. He probably sensed that Reggie was about as "salty" as a man could be. And Reggie thought that Seaweed was the perfect first mate. As I shut the lights and lay down on my cot I thought how, in a sea-faring life, you sometimes make friends in the strangest ways.

Chapter Thirteen

☙

THE LOCAL NEWSPAPER said that divers scoured the floor of the bay and found pieces of the mine. This evidence was matched with first-hand accounts by the jet-skiers, who said they saw the submariner trying to pull the mine out to sea. The jet-skiers, just twelve- and thirteen-year-olds, said they thought the submariner was very brave but had been injured by the blast. And so, what started out as a search for an attacking foreign submarine, turned into the story of a heroic, solitary submariner sailing the seas for the cause of justice. "The people of Graciosa feel a debt of gratitude to the lonely submariner, and dearly hope he is not suffering too much from his wounds . . . ," read the morning paper, as translated by Reggie.

"Now you are a local hero, Alfred. Now we can walk through the village proudly and eat in the café for free."

He chuckled.

"No, thanks. I think I'll keep my presence a secret."

I had been in the newspaper before and knew just how easily they could change the way people thought about you. I had also learned that news stories were like movies — they tried to make them as entertaining as possible and didn't care too much whether they were really true or not. Reggie went on to read, for instance, that the submariner had been identified as a Swiss national, because the jet-skiers said that his flag was red and white — someone said a white cross on a red background. When that claim was contested on the basis of Switzerland being a land-locked country, it was defended by the fact that it was also a "neutral" country, the home of the Red Cross, Saint Bernard dogs and a reputation for rescuing people.

"Well," said Reggie, "you can't argue with that. I guess you're from Switzerland."

I was just glad that the chase had been called off and that I could sneak out of the bay at night without being seen. But I ended up hanging around for a few days anyway, because it was fun. Like me, Reggie was nocturnal. He liked to sleep after the sun came up, sleep into the late afternoon and stay up all night. Occasionally, like me, he would change his sleeping schedule to enjoy the day. One of his favourite things to do in the Azores, he said, was to take a hike into the hills, find one of the hot springs and have a soak. It was good for the body and good for the mind. So that's what we did. It was particularly exciting for Hollie, who seemed to understand perfectly that we were out for a walk of considerable length, and paced himself well and drank plenty of water. Seaweed, on the other hand, joined us for about five minutes. Then he took to the air and probably went to the dump.

Graciosa is beautiful. It is a little bit like Newfoundland because it is rocky, but a lot greener. There are small farms and green fields and treed hills. The biggest difference is that it is a lot warmer. As we climbed into the hills, with a great view of the island and sea, we worked up a heavy sweat. Hollie was panting.

"It's not too much further," said Reggie, "and believe me, it's more than worth it."

The trail led to a small lake on top of a hill, which had once been a volcano. Beside the lake were the hot springs — small pools of water that flowed up from deep within the earth's crust. Some of them were so hot you had to be careful where you stepped. We stripped down to our shorts, stepped slowly into the water and found comfortable spots to lie down. After a few minutes of getting used to it, I thought it was the nicest feeling in the world. Hollie sniffed at the water, licked it, pawed it, barked at it, then finally settled down in a shady spot and went to sleep. It had been quite a hike for him.

"So, Alfred," said Reggie, "where to from here? Where do you go next and what do you intend to do?"

Reggie talked with his eyes closed and his toes sticking out of the water.

"I'm looking for Atlantis."

"Really?"

"Yah, sort of. I mean, nobody knows if it really exists or not. But if it does, it's probably in Greece somewhere. Some people say it might be around here, but more likely it's off the island of Thera, in the Mediterranean. That's where Jacques Cousteau went looking for it."

"Did he find it?"

"He found lots of broken pots and statues and stuff. But that might have been dumped out of ships. Nobody knows for sure."

"Interesting. I don't think it's around here. Nobody ever talks about it here. But they do talk about it on the Med. And you're a lot more likely to run into mermaids there. And that says something."

I raised my head. "Do you believe in mermaids?"

"It's not so much whether I *believe* in mermaids or not — there's definitely something there — it's more a question of *what* they are. But if you asked me twenty years ago I would have said you were crazy."

"And now?"

"Now I believe in something, but I can't say what it is. Let me put it this way: the longer you stay at sea, the more you realize you are not alone."

"Oh. What else is there?"

"Well, ghosts, for one. All the sailors I know who circumnavigate the globe, and it's a more regular group than you might imagine, have ghosts appear on their boats from time to time. Some keep regular company with them."

"With ghosts? Really?"

"Yes indeed. The sea is a tragic and lonely place, Alfred. I mean, there are those of us who wouldn't be anywhere else, who *couldn't* be anywhere else — I kind of suspect you're a bit like that — but when all is said and done, it's a tragic and lonely place, and that just draws the ghosts."

"Oh. And mermaids?"

"Well, now that's a different kettle of fish altogether. Mermaids aren't scary creatures or anything, and I don't believe they're out to pull a man to his death, like some people believe, but I think they're kind of mischievous."

"Have you ever seen one?"

"I can't say that I have, but I've heard them, and it's not a particularly nice sound. It's very screechy."

"That's what my friend says."

I was surprised how similar Reggie's and Sheba's descriptions of mermaids were.

"If you sail around the Mediterranean long enough I'm pretty sure you'll hear mermaids for yourself. Have you been on the Med before?"

"Nope."

"Well, you're going to love it. And the Greek islands . . . just heavenly. But I don't think anybody's allowed to dive in

Greek waters without government authority, which is probably impossible to get."

"I know. I'm not planning to dive for anything, just to look. I won't touch anything."

"But what if you see a treasure?"

"I guess I'd report it."

"Sounds pretty exciting. Maybe you'll see mermaids. I've got half a mind to go back there myself. How are you going to get through the Strait of Gibraltar with your submarine?"

"I'm pretty sneaky."

"This I can believe."

"But I obey the Convention on the Law of the Sea . . . mostly."

"The Convention?"

"Yah."

"I see. And what about pirates?"

"I've never run into any. Have you?"

"Oh, yes! Vicious, vicious characters! If you ever see pirates, Alfred, slip beneath the waves and sail away as fast as you can. Pirates don't care how old you are; they don't care about anything except what they can steal from you and how they can hurt you."

"Have they ever stolen anything from you?"

"Lots! Many times! But what really scared me was seeing a sailboat after it had been attacked by pirates and all its crew killed."

"Killed? Really?"

"Cut to pieces."

"Oh my gosh!"

"Yup. The whole deck was covered in blood. Made me sick to my stomach. Everything bad you ever heard about pirates is true, and worse!"

"But I think I should be pretty safe in my submarine."

"I think so. But be careful. What you want to watch out for is a sailboat that looks like it is in trouble but isn't. That's one of their tricks. They'll be waving a white flag and looking distressed. Then, when you get close enough they'll open fire on you and take your sub. More than likely they'll kill you."

"But how can you know? What if it really is a sailboat in distress?"

"You should be able to tell if you keep your eyes open. Take a darn good look with your binoculars before you get too close. Ask them to identify themselves and bring the whole crew on deck. If you get the slightest sense of anything suspicious, stay away, and call the authorities."

I appreciated the advice from such a seasoned sailor. I hoped I'd never run into pirates. If I did, I hoped my premonition feeling would be working.

After three days it was time to return to sea. We went out together, sailboat and submarine, just five miles or so. Reggie and Seaweed sailed above, Hollie and I directly below so that we would appear as one beep on anyone's radar screen, even though there was no longer a radar net in place. When

I heard Reggie cut his motor, I cut ours and brought the sub up beside the boat. It was the middle of the night; we were all wide-awake.

"This is as far as we go for now, young captain," said Reggie. "But I've got a feeling we'll meet again some day. The sea has a way of bringing good friends together again."

"I hope so," I said. And I really did.

Reggie stood up and saluted me. I saluted back. He started his engine and turned around. I felt sad watching him go. He looked so alone. He lived all alone. He didn't even have a crew, like I did. Speaking of which . . . Seaweed was still on his boat. As they disappeared into the darkness I started to wonder . . . then heard a familiar call and my first mate flew back to the sub.

"Goodbye, Reggie!" I called out.

"Goodbye, mate! Keep your eyes peeled for pirates!"

I would indeed.

Chapter Fourteen

❦

THE WIND CURLED UP the corners of Hollie's mouth and made Seaweed work to keep up as we approached the Portuguese coast. Both needed the fresh air; we had been submerged too long. It had been a rough, four-day sail from the Azores. We had stayed on the surface only long enough to charge the batteries, about four or five hours at a time, then dove and enjoyed the peace and calm at one hundred feet. I got a lot of exercise pedalling but it was a long time for a dog and seagull to stay cooped up. Hollie had enjoyed our hike in the Azores and was anxious to do it again. I wasn't sure when I could make that happen but would try.

We were about twenty miles from land, still in international waters, when I thought I heard the radar beep. I went inside. Nope, nothing on the radar screen. I climbed back up the portal. Hollie was still under my arm. Once again, I thought I heard the radar beep. The wind was strong. Occasionally we would hear Seaweed squawk above us, but the radar beep was a very particular sound, nothing like a seagull. I went back inside and watched the screen. Nothing. Soon there would be north-south sea traffic along the coast, I imagined, just like back home, but so far, nothing. I climbed the portal one more time, raised my hand to block the sun and . . . was that something in the water directly ahead? . . . BANG!!! We hit something! We collided with something floating just beneath the surface. The force of impact almost knocked me out of the portal backwards. I only had one hand free to grip the hatch; the other hand was holding Hollie, and I squeezed him so tightly he yelped. The sub was rocking back and forth trying to push whatever it was out of the way. I rushed inside and shut off the engine. I took a quick look in the bow to see if there was a leak. Nope. I put Hollie down and went back out. Lying in the water in front of us was a full-length container, the kind they lift on and off trains and stack on top of freighters. They stack them by the hundreds without tying them down and it is common for a ship to lose a few in a storm. Most sink, but they can float, depending upon what they are carrying. Then they become extremely dangerous to sailboats and other vessels. No wonder the radar was beeping irregularly. In a large wave, part of the container probably stuck out of the water and the radar picked it up, then, it disappeared again.

I strapped on the harness, climbed out onto the bow and looked for a dent. There was a big tear in the container, but I couldn't find a dent in the sub. Ziegfried's ingenious design allowed the sub to take a hit without denting easily. It was like a steel ball with a wooden core and a rubber layer between, which would bounce when it hit something.

I had two thoughts: that I wanted to know what was in the container — after all, it was anyone's for the taking now — and that I should try to sink it, so that it wouldn't collide with another vessel.

I waited for a while to see if the tear we had created would sink the container. I didn't want to tie up to it if it were going to the bottom of the sea. After an hour or so, it hadn't sunk any deeper. It was floating with its top just on the surface, so that you could walk across it, although waves washed over it. I tied the sub loosely to two corners, so that if the container did suddenly plunge to the bottom, I could quickly undo the ropes. Then, I tied a longer rope to my harness and climbed out to take a closer look.

The tear was near the top. I saw a cardboard box caught in the ripped metal and the box was light enough to float. I jumped onto the container, crouched down and held onto the edge of it with my hands as I made my way over to the tear. If a wooden or fiberglass sailboat ever struck a container like this it would shatter its hull and sink in a hurry. What a dangerous way to transport things!

Bending down, I couldn't reach the tear. I had to jump into the water. It wasn't too cold but the waves were pressing the sub and container together. I would just take a quick peek and get out of there. I reached the tear, gripped the wet cardboard box and pulled it apart. Out streamed little girl's dolls wrapped in plastic. They floated. Was the container filled with *toys*?

As far as I could tell, about two feet of air was trapped inside the container, and it was filled with floating boxes. I tried to see deeper inside but it was too dark, so I went back to the sub for a flashlight and gaff. The gaff was five feet long, with a hook on one end. With my arm outstretched, I could reach about eight feet. I jumped back into the water, hooked my harness rope around the jagged metal of the tear, stuck the gaff into the hole with one hand and turned on the flashlight with the other. The flashlight showed hundreds of boxes jammed tightly against the top of the container. That's what was keeping it afloat. I grabbed hold of another box with the gaff and gave it a tug. The wet cardboard came apart easily and small toys in plastic packages came floating towards me and went out the hole. There were squirt guns, balls, yo-yos, toy guns, baby dolls, Frisbees, skipping ropes, and so on, all made out of plastic or rubber and all floating. It was such a strange feeling seeing the toys float by, as if Santa Claus' bag had fallen out of his sleigh when he was flying over the ocean. I felt an urge to grab the toys so that they wouldn't be wasted but there were too many of them. And what would I do with them? Where would I keep them? Then the light of the flashlight fell across pictures on the sides of other boxes and I saw two things that I really did want: motorized toy boats and pellet-rifles. I figured the motorized boats would come in handy somehow. And the pellet rifles? Well . . . I had always wanted one, and never got one.

Problem was, those boxes were wedged in tightly on the far side of the container. I tried to dislodge them by pulling on some other boxes, but it didn't work. Lots of boxes drifted past me and went out the hole. If I wanted the guns and boats I had to climb inside the container, and that was just not a good idea. I knew it wasn't a good idea. I even said out loud that it wasn't a good idea. I said it loudly as I climbed inside and reached out with the gaff. The guns and boats weren't far away; I just had to reach . . . but my weight shifted the balance of the container. It tilted suddenly and I dropped the flashlight. Now I couldn't see, except for the light around the hole, but that was partly blocked by the boxes drifting out of it. I should have paid attention to that too, because that was changing the buoyancy of the container. I just wanted those guns and boats so much, and I was almost there . . . just a little further . . . and . . . the container started to sink!

One would think that a sinking container would be enough to make anyone panic and forget about a couple of toys, but I made one last desperate lunge for the box of pellet rifles, and in so doing, wedged my rope tightly into the jagged metal of the hole. I took a deep breath as the two feet of air in the container was very suddenly replaced with sea-water and the whole thing no longer had any reason to stay afloat. On one hand, it was great that I didn't panic; panick-'ing at sea is always dangerous. On the other hand, I had grown a little too comfortable in such situations, knowing I could hold my breath for two full minutes. That wouldn't help me much at the bottom of the sea.

As the rope grew taut, the container, the toys and myself, began to descend. Still, I knew there was a small safety fea-ture in the fact that the container was moored to the sub by two of its corners, even if just loosely. Surely the sub's buoy-ancy would keep the container from sinking more than a few feet. What I hadn't foreseen was that I had tied the two ropes to the top of the portal, so that as the container started down, it merely pulled the sub over.

It was, in fact, about to pull it upside-down! Suddenly I thought of Hollie and flung myself out the hole. The rope was caught but I pulled it with all my might. I had one sec-ond of panic before I was able to pull it free. Looking up about ten feet, I saw the sub being pulled down onto its side. I reached one side of the container and freed one of the ropes. I was now about fifteen feet below the surface and the side of the portal was just about touching the surface. Waves must have been rushing inside the sub. I reached the other rope and pulled hard. Please! Please, let go! Slowly, but what felt like forever, the rope loosened from the other corner. I let it go. The sub was on its side. I stared up at it, nearly twenty feet above me. Boxes kept floating out of the container and drifting up past me. "Please right!" I said to the sub, begging . . . and then it did.

As I swam up to the surface, I looked down and watched the container slowly disappear beneath me. I wondered how far it would fall before the pressure would flatten it like a tin can. I swam over to the sub and climbed up.

"Are you okay in there, Hollie?"

I heard his excited bark. Thank Heavens he was okay. I looked up in the sky and saw Seaweed gazing down, probably wondering what the heck I was doing. I waved.

"It's okay, Seaweed," I shouted. "Just a stupid mistake."

"Stupid" hardly described it. *What* was I thinking?

Toys in plastic packages littered the surface where the container had gone down. Everything not airtight in plastic went to the bottom of the sea. Lucky for me the pellet-rifles, with their wooden shafts, were plastic-wrapped. I found six of them. I inflated the rubber dinghy and Hollie and I paddled around picking up toys until we had made quite a pile of them in the dinghy. I didn't know what to do with the toys but couldn't leave them. We also retrieved eight motorized toy boats, made of tin, each about ten inches long. Hollie was very pleased to get his jaws around a rubber ball. Even Seaweed got involved in the cleanup, dropping out of the sky and picking up brightly coloured packages in his beak and tossing them into the portal. He had remarkably good aim.

But I didn't feel that I deserved the toys for which I had

foolishly risked all of our lives. At twenty miles from the coast Seaweed would likely have survived but Hollie and I would have perished, had I not escaped the sinking container. For a little while it seemed like the right thing to do was to punish myself by denying myself the pleasure of playing with the pellet-rifles. But I could not resist opening one, removing the little pouch of pellets taped to the butt of the gun, pumping the gun and shooting it. Then, I tied an empty can on top of a couple of balloons, set it adrift and practised shooting. The gun ripped holes through the can as if it were paper. Then I shot the balloons. I would have to find another way to punish myself; the guns were simply too much fun.

Somehow, I found space for all the toys we picked up. I stuffed them into the corners and recesses of the sub. Some went into the engine compartment, some under the floor and some under the mattress on my bed. Hollie was tickled pink with his rubber ball and played with it continually. Seaweed tried a couple of times to catch it but there was no way Hollie would let him near it. He even knew it by name. If I said, "Where's the ball?" he would immediately appear with it. But he wouldn't give it to me.

We were approaching the coast of Portugal about two hundred miles north of Lisbon, as far as I could tell. Fifteen miles from shore we picked up the first vessel on radar, then a second one, then a whole bunch! I steered south in an arc and blended in with a steady stream of sea traffic. The ships sailing north kept closer to shore than those sailing south. I tried to keep at least five miles from any other vessel and turned on our lights. It was better to hide by looking just like any other ship — a distant light on the water.

But keeping five miles away from other vessels proved harder than I thought. Some were faster than others. I kept an eye on the radar and tried not to let any ship get close enough to identify us. I wanted everyone to think we were just another sailboat sailing to the Mediterranean for a vacation, not a submarine from Newfoundland searching for Atlantis.

The trickiest thing was crossing the lines of traffic and submerging to sleep. To any ship watching their radar closely it would look like we had sunk. I crossed the lane at the speed of a sailboat, looked for a bay with other boats in the water and submerged. I doubted anyone would trace our movement into a bay, count how many boats were moored in the bay, then notice that one light had just vanished from their screen. But it was possible.

I carried Hollie up the portal for one last breath of air before going down to sleep. Portugal loomed in front of us like a sleeping giant. Lights spread out across the hills like fireflies. The sun would soon be up. Hollie held his nose sharply in the air. He could smell land.

"Soon, Hollie," I said. "Soon."

Chapter Fifteen

IT FELT AS IF WE were a soap bubble swirling around and around before going through the bathtub drain. Dozens of ships, large and small, were merging from north and south towards the funnel that was the Strait of Gibraltar. The thicker the traffic at the top of the funnel, the harder it was for us to stay on the surface, until, finally, we couldn't anymore. As the sun rose and the nearest ship closed to two miles, we submerged. We disappeared from sight and radar. We really had no choice. I supposed we could have sailed on the surface with our flags all quite legally, since we were still outside the twelve-mile zone of any country, but passing through the Strait would bring us within the legal jurisdiction of both Britain and Spain, and somebody would surely want to know what business we had coming into the Mediterranean.

The Strait of Gibraltar is a narrow channel between Europe and Africa. The northern side belongs to Spain, except for the very bottom tip, which is owned by Britain — a sore spot for Spain. The southern side belongs to Morocco, except for the top corner, which is owned by Spain — a sore spot for Morocco. At its narrowest point the Strait is only eight miles wide. But it's one thousand feet deep. The top three hundred feet has a strong current pouring into the Mediterranean from the Atlantic. The bottom seven hundred feet is pouring back out! And the space where the two currents meet is a wave, just like on the surface, except that it's three hundred feet below! Military submarines leaving the Mediterranean submerge below the wave, shut everything off and drift out with the current, silent and undetected. Subs coming in do the same, *above* the wave. Well, that sounded easy enough. We would behave just like any other submarine pretending not to be there.

But I needed to sleep first. On battery power I steered towards shallower water. Morocco seemed a better choice than Spain because they didn't have as powerful a navy, nor were they in an angry dispute with Canada. By mid-morning we settled on the bottom at two hundred and fifty feet, ten miles offshore from Tangiers. I shut everything off and fell into a blissful sleep. The last thing I heard was Hollie sigh.

We ate a nice breakfast. I treated the crew to tuna fish sandwiches made with buttered bread. I cut them into small bites. Then I opened a can of stinky wet dog food. The crew got excited but I had to hold my nose. We were not going to surface at all for a whole day; I wanted to keep them happy.

To join the stream of traffic I started to pedal, keeping the sub at two hundred and fifty feet. Four hours later I steered into the current, shut the sonar off and let the current pull us through the Strait like a leaf down a river. I made myself comfortable with a cup of tea and a playful dog at my feet. Hollie was preoccupied with the splayed end of a piece of rope. He was so wrapped up in it he didn't even notice Seaweed pecking at his rubber ball, and I didn't tell him. If Seaweed destroyed the ball, I would just give him another one. We had about seventeen or so in the engine compartment.

Slowly and silently we drifted through the channel, deaf, dumb and blind. I kept the sonar off so that anyone listening with sensitive equipment wouldn't hear its pings. It was quiet and still, yet I found myself biting my nails and sighing a lot. It was so quiet it was unnerving. Without sonar we couldn't even tell if we were actually moving, though I knew we were. We simply had to wait. But it seemed to take forever. When I thought we must have been about halfway through, I checked the clock. Only three hours had passed! Now, whenever I sighed, Hollie sighed. Seaweed was in a deep sleep. I tried to read a book but couldn't concentrate. If only I could turn on the sonar I would have something to watch and some way to know where we were and how fast we were drifting. But I couldn't risk giving our presence away.

And then we hit something.

It struck the bow on the starboard side. It didn't hit terribly hard but it scared the heck out of me. It was loud. It was a loud hollow scraping sound, as if we had gently bounced off something — a container perhaps? We weren't drifting very fast, maybe three nautical miles per hour, but likely faster than whatever we hit, because of our dolphin nose and streamlined shape. At least I could tell that we were drifting forwards instead of backwards or sideways, because the object had struck close to the bow. If we were spinning in circles I was pretty sure I'd be able to tell by the feel of it.

The minutes passed like hours, and then we struck something else! This time we hit it dead on, and I heard it drag down the starboard side. Suddenly I had a frightening thought: we were obviously striking objects smaller than the sub — debris perhaps, fallen from ships, like the container we had sunk in the Atlantic. But what if there were mines out there? It had happened in the Azores.

I couldn't stand it anymore. I decided to turn on the sonar for ten seconds then shut it off I sat down in front of the screen, planning not to blink for ten seconds. I would scan the area immediately around us, determine our depth and try to gauge our speed. If anyone picked up our sonar wave they would only have ten seconds to locate us. By then we would have disappeared again. Perhaps they would think their reading was just a mistake. Sonar was hardly a perfect science.

I flicked the switch and the screen came alive. There was debris all around us! The Strait looked like a garbage dump under water. No wonder we had struck a couple of objects. We were drifting about three nautical miles per hour, as predicted in my mariner's manual. I didn't have time to look closely at everything but I did notice what looked like a long object several hundred feet below drifting in the opposite direction — a military submarine? Probably. In any case, we were hardly alone. There were at least a dozen vessels above, sailing in all directions, in, out and across the Strait. Just before I shut off the screen I read the sea floor depth — one thousand feet. I sat back in my seat. It occurred to me that if there were a mine in the Strait, which was unlikely anyway, it would almost certainly not be drifting at two hundred and fifty feet. I watched Hollie playing with his ball. That seemed like a wise thing to do. I went into the engine compartment and got three for myself. I decided to take my mind off the rest of the time by learning how to juggle.

Fifteen hours later I still couldn't juggle, but we had entered the mouth of the Mediterranean. Thank Heavens! We had struck a few more objects on the way through but they were small, and none of them exploded. Rising to the surface for the first time in twenty-two hours, I opened the hatch to a starry sky. Seaweed went out of the portal like a spark from a fire. Even Hollie couldn't wait, and started to climb on his own, until I scooped him up and carried him out.

We stood in the portal with our noses pointed south. The air was soft and sweet. It was the strangest thing but I really thought I could smell all kinds of things in the air — flowers, honey, wheat, hay . . . hot sand? Strangest of all, it was a dry air. Here we were surrounded by water, but the air we breathed was dry in our throats. I didn't know how that could be but it was a pleasant dryness.

I started up the engine and headed southeast. I wanted to reach the Moroccan coast before the sun rose and get Hollie out for a run on the beach. The coast stretched out before us from Morocco, Algeria, Tunisia, Libya, as far east as Egypt. I couldn't believe it; we had sailed from northern Newfoundland all the way to the continent of Africa!

Chapter Sixteen

SOMETIMES GREAT danger is lurking beneath a gentle mask.

The water along the coast was only fifty feet deep in places. After crossing the Atlantic, that seemed like nothing. At fifty feet there was nowhere to hide from the air, although I wasn't really expecting helicopters. I didn't know what to expect, actually, except that if we landed on the beach and climbed over the mountains we would find ourselves in the Sahara, the biggest desert in the world!

In the dark I chose a small bay, submerged to periscope depth and motored in until we were in only ten feet of water. The periscope showed no lights on the beach so I surfaced, opened the hatch, dropped our little anchor and inflated the dinghy. If we saw anyone we would run back to the sub and leave.

Hollie and I paddled to shore. Seaweed was standing on the beach already waiting for us. It was an exciting moment, stepping out of the dinghy onto the continent of Africa. Since there were no houses, power-lines, telephone poles, roads, bridges or signs of human habitation whatsoever, it was easy to imagine we were the first ones to discover the continent, though I knew *that* wasn't true.

I put Hollie down and watched him run wild in the sand while Seaweed hopped up and down and flapped his wings. Hollie went around and around in circles until I got dizzy watching him. Then he broke the circle and ran all the way down the beach. I followed him. Hollie was a sailor dog through and through. I had found him on the sea, and he was spending his life there, but he sure did love to get out on land and run.

We were about half a mile down the beach when the sun came over the horizon and transformed everything into a golden haze. The air, the sea, the land, all of it changed instantly and became so bright it was almost blinding. Unlike the Atlantic, which was dark and gray, the Mediterranean was light green and sparkled in the sun. It was warmer too when I stepped in it, and saltier when I tasted it. The sand was also lighter and I wondered if that was because the sun had baked it so much. I used to think sand was just sand, but the sand here looked as if it had been painted by the sun.

I sat down and sifted my fingers through the sand and thought of things I had read about this place. Two thousand years ago there were lions on these beaches. The Romans caught them and shipped them across the sea to Rome for bloodthirsty entertainment in their coliseum. Now there were none. Ten thousand years ago the Sahara was a jungle. There were great rivers running through it like a spider's web. That was hard to believe. The rivers are still there, scientists claim. They flow deep beneath the sand. When I thought about these things, Atlantis didn't seem quite so far-fetched.

It was time to sleep. I stood up and turned to go back down the beach, then saw something really weird. There was an orange cloud rolling onto the beach from the direction of the desert. The strange thing was, I didn't feel any wind. And then, I did! And it was coming fast!

I had never seen an orange cloud before. It wasn't like a normal cloud. It was low, close to the ground and moving like a snake. But why was it orange? In less than a minute I had my answer.

Sand.

I thought sandstorms were things you only found in the desert, not on a beach. Oh well, I thought, it would be interesting to watch. Another minute later I realized something else — you didn't *watch* a sandstorm, you got the heck out of the way! The sand in the cloud was a lot finer than the sand on the beach. It was more like a powder, and it quickly started filling my nose, mouth, ears and eyes. My eyes dried out immediately and I couldn't blink. My throat started to dry and I found it hard to breathe. Suddenly, I couldn't see anything!

Still, it took me awhile to realize how dangerous the situation was. I thought it was just a small cloud that was going to pass in a few minutes. I shut my eyes, held my breath and covered my ears with my hands. Hollie started to whimper.

"It's okay, Hollie," I mumbled. "It'll pass in a minute."

But it didn't. We had to get out of there. I pulled my t-shirt over my head, reached down and picked up Hollie. I started to run, but couldn't even find the sea! I went this way and that, gagging with the dry powder in my throat, until I felt water under my feet. I figured out the right direction, held Hollie's face inside my t-shirt with mine and ran as fast as I could down the beach. I kept kicking my feet into the water to make sure I was going the right way.

It took forever to find the dinghy. Instead of blowing away, the dinghy was being buried in the sand. I turned it over and we crawled underneath. That didn't help much. The fine sand got in everywhere! Hollie kept his eyes closed but he was orange with sand, and it wasn't the kind of sand you could shake off, it stuck to you. I pulled the dinghy to the water, climbed in and paddled out. But I couldn't find the sub!

"Come on!" I yelled. "Where *are* you?"

The wind was so strong it blew us quickly from shore. I couldn't even paddle against it. If I didn't find the sub, the sandstorm was going to blow us out to sea! I had to think fast. I left Hollie in the dinghy, jumped into the water and held onto the rope. My body acted as a kind of anchor and slowed the dinghy down. Then I slipped under the surface and looked for the sub. It was a lot easier to see under water, though I couldn't hold my breath long because I couldn't take a deep enough breath to start. But I found the sub, pulled the dinghy over and we climbed inside.

I gave Hollie some fresh water. He scratched at his eyes with his paws, the poor thing. I took a drink of water and threw up. Still, it was a huge relief to get inside. There was just one big problem: where was Seaweed?

I sat and thought about it. It made sense to think that he had flown out to sea and stayed ahead of the sandstorm. Maybe that's what he did. The only trouble with that idea was that seagulls, as a rule, bedded down on the beach during a storm. They let the wind roar over them and waited it out. They didn't go to sea. I didn't know how far out to sea this sand was blowing, or how far I'd have to sail to be able to see through it to find him. And if he hadn't gone out to sea and was stuck on the beach, it would be a long time before I'd be back. Would he survive a sandstorm? I thought of how quickly the sand had been covering the dinghy. I had to go back!

I pulled the anchor free, started the engine and motored in as close to the beach as I dared. I shut off the engine, dropped anchor again, grabbed a long rope, went out and closed the hatch from the outside. I took a jacket this time. After tying the rope to the portal, I jumped overboard and swam underwater to the beach, with the rope in one hand. I wrapped the wet jacket around my head and fought my way up the beach against the wind. It wasn't howling the way storms normally do; it was more of a steady roar, like a jet engine.

I wasn't expecting to find Seaweed by looking. I was hoping that if he heard me yelling his name, he would squawk, and I would follow the sound and locate him. And so I went around yelling as loud as I possibly could, with the jacket in front of my face. I refused to give up.

When I finally heard his squawk, it was weak. He had turned himself into the wind, just as I thought he would. But he had to keep shifting himself around because the sand kept trying to bury him. He was exhausted when I found him. Such a tough bird to have survived!

It was the only time Seaweed ever let me pick him up. It was the only time I ever tried. He didn't like it. But I ran around until I found the water again, and then the rope, and then the sub. And I was so happy.

We motored out a few miles and settled on the bottom at seventy-five feet. I floated the antenna and turned the radio on low. A different kind of music entered the sub now — wooden flutes and drums and voices. I sat on the floor by the observation window and helped the crew clean the sand from their fur and feathers. After such a crazy and violent storm, the peace and calm inside the sub was heavenly. The music was peaceful. I didn't know what language it was but the voices were of children, and they sounded happy. After I fed the crew and had a cup of tea, I lay down on my bed and fell asleep listening to it.

Chapter Seventeen

⟨∽⟩

I WOKE TO THE sound of drums. There was humming and singing and funny clicking sounds people were making with their throats. It was cool. I tried to imitate it, although Seaweed gawked at me, wondering what the heck I was doing. He seemed distressed.

"I'm trying to learn something new, Seaweed."

Seaweed would eat absolutely anything but was surprisingly fussy about what he would listen to. When we surfaced and I opened the hatch, he twisted his head from the bottom of the portal, peeked up at the sky suspiciously, then bolted up and out the hatch. I was glad to see he had fully recovered.

It was a clear sky, not quite twilight. We were five miles from shore. There was no sign of a storm having passed at all. It came and went too quickly to have any effect on the waves or current. Through the binoculars I could tell that the beach was clear. There were no vessels moving around, according to radar, and nothing coming our way. I decided to cruise down the coast, keeping a constant distance from shore. I raised the Canadian flag to sail legally on the surface by "right of safe passage." When the sun went down I would turn on our lights.

We were heading east with the shore always on the starboard. From five miles you could see the mountains. Unlike in Canada, where mountains were usually green or white above a gray-brown shore, these mountains were reddish-brown above green foothills. Occasionally there were snow-caps. Beyond the mountains was the desert, which I wished we could have seen. I wondered how the sandstorm had reached the beach all the way from the desert. It couldn't have come over the mountains. There must have been a gorge or canyon where the wind snaked through at high speed. Perhaps it was an old riverbed. Now I understood how a jungle could turn into a desert. All I had to do was remember the sandstorm, which had lasted only a few hours, then multiply that by a thousand years. The Sahara was big enough to swallow ten Newfoundlands, and was still growing, according to scientists. I tried to imagine ten Newfoundlands hidden beneath sand. Suddenly the thought of losing an island didn't seem so incredible. You could probably bury one in just a few days.

For three days we sailed without trouble and took long walks on the beach without incident. But after three days my premonition feeling came back.

Algiers lay ahead, fifteen miles. I was picking up vessels on radar. As I stood and stared at the screen and watched the movement of boats in the water outside the city, I started to get a strange feeling; I had no idea why. Sheba had insisted I trust those feelings. Okay, but it was weird. I had no reason to suspect anything. There were always recreational boaters around a port city. Maybe it was something in the way some of them were moving, as if they were on patrol. Three boats always moved together, turning in the same direction at the same time. Well, I had no intention of exploring Algiers anyway.

It was around ten o'clock. The sun had just gone down. I coaxed Seaweed inside and was about to slip beneath the surface. We would switch to battery power, disappear from radar and continue on our course. How likely was it those boats would be set up with sonar?

We would be sailing illegally once we submerged. The Law of the Sea allowed submarines "right of innocent passage" only on the surface. I stared at the screen and hesitated. The problem with a premonition feeling was that there was no logical sense to it, no reason. It was just a feeling. On one hand, it was a good feeling when I knew we were sailing legally. On the other hand, local officials had every right to stop us, inspect our vessel, even require us to dock for several days or longer while they closely investigated the sub. They could even refuse us permission to continue sailing if they felt like it.

I was still mulling over the whole thing when I realized we were already within their radar range. They knew we were there. Well, that settled it. I switched on our lights and continued our course. They would not be able to see us anyway unless they examined every radar beep with a powerful telescope, in the dark, and what were the chances they would do *that*?

Pretty good, as it turned out. We were passing the city, five miles from shore, just one of a number of smaller vessels in the water, and we had our lights on. There was no reason to radio local authorities because we were not coming in to dock. The only way they would know we were not a sailboat or motorboat, was if they took a visual look at us. As I kept my eyes glued to the radar screen, I saw those three boats suddenly veer in our direction. Since there was no other vessel in our immediate area, I had to assume they were coming towards us! What to do?

We couldn't outrun them; they were too fast. We had either to wait and meet them, and risk being taken in for inspection, or submerge and try to slip away. I quickly climbed the portal and watched the approaching boats through the binoculars. There were three or four men in uniform in each boat. They were staring at us with binoculars too, and they were carrying machine guns! Suddenly, I got a *very* bad feeling about the whole thing.

"We're going down!" I yelled to the crew.

I shut the hatch and let water into the tanks. We started to dive. But as we were sailing in only a hundred and fifty feet of water, we couldn't dive very deeply. I switched to battery power and headed straight out to sea. I watched the three boats approach on sonar. When they were a quarter of a mile away, I made a sharp right turn. I wanted to see if they were following us with sonar. They turned. They were! Yikes!

I straightened out and headed due north, the shortest route to leave the twelve-mile zone. I wondered how far they would chase us. Would they respect the twelve-mile zone? And then . . . there was an explosion in the water! It was pretty loud but didn't rock the sub. It was nothing like the mine that blew up in the Azores. It sounded more like a firecracker. I watched the sea floor closely and followed it down its gradual descent. Another mile out and we were down to two hundred feet. There was another explosion. Again it was loud but not very threatening. It was more like a warning blast. They were just motorboats; they were not equipped to deal with submarines, surely? I was guessing what they were doing was throwing hand grenades in the water, trying to force us to surface. But the grenades were exploding before they fell very far and were not affecting us at all. There was no way I would surface now and attempt a meeting with them. The time for nice greetings had passed. They were attempting either to sink us or force us to surface, as if we were a hostile enemy. If they caught us now they would surely put me in jail, and probably keep me there for a very long time. Ziegfried had said, never get put into jail in a third world country, because you'll never get out. And what would have happened to Hollie and Seaweed?

Another mile out and we were down to two hundred and thirty feet. They were right above us, dropping grenades still, to no effect. Perhaps it was fun for them, a little chase on a quiet summer's night and a chance to practise throwing grenades.

After another mile the sea floor took a sudden drop of a hundred feet. I submerged to three hundred feet. The explosions grew weaker. I wondered how far they would chase us. Would they stop at the twelve-mile zone? At ten miles from shore they stopped throwing grenades. Sonar revealed another vessel in the water, possibly a passing freighter. One of the motorboats left the others to sail alongside of it, probably checking it out. We reached eleven miles . . . eleven and a half . . . twelve! I watched on the sonar screen as the remaining two boats swung around in wide arcs and headed back. I took a deep breath and sighed. We had escaped. Once again, Sheba had been right!

Chapter Eighteen

✍

CHASED AWAY FROM the African coast, we headed north. We could have sailed in an arc and gradually made our way back, east of Algiers, but something directly ahead interested me — the island of Mallorca. My guidebook said it was famous for wild mountain goats. I wanted to see them.

We surfaced and I switched on the radar. No one was following us anymore. I climbed the portal and opened the hatch. Seaweed went out. I carried Hollie up and we made ourselves comfortable and watched the stars.

I had seen pictures of mountain goats. They were large, thickly furred, heavy-looking beasts that could run up and down the sides of cliffs as if they had wings on their feet. It was amazing. There were lots of goats on Mallorca, according to the book, and it was only a day's sail away. The only snag was that Mallorca belonged to Spain, not exactly the best of friends with Canada at the moment.

We sailed through the night and reached the twelve-mile zone of Mallorca by mid-morning. Radar revealed ships sailing in and out of the main harbour like wasps around a nest. That made it a lot easier. With so much sea traffic, no one would notice us, so long as we stayed out of sight. We submerged to periscope depth and sailed around the west side.

I began to search for places to hide. I wanted to find a small cove where we could leave the sub long enough to take a hike into the mountains, maybe even camp overnight. I knew that was ambitious, especially on a highly populated island, but there must have been rocky areas where no one lived? Every island had them.

Cruising along the coast less than a quarter of a mile from shore, I found lots of rocky areas, but the coves always seemed to have boats in them, or people. By this time, I was getting sleepy. Finally, I found one cove that looked hopeful. It was isolated and surrounded by cliffs. There was nobody on the beach. I motored in, let Seaweed out, submerged to seventy-five feet and settled down to get some sleep.

When we woke and came up to periscope level there was a man sitting on the beach. It was just one man and he was alone in the little cove, a sheltered cove, the perfect place to hide the sub, but we would have to wait until he left.

I fed Hollie and made tea and fiddled about while we waited. When Hollie finished eating he was anxious to go for a walk. He followed me around and stared up at the hatch as if to say, what's the holdup?

"Sorry, Hollie. There's a man out there."

I kept peeking through the periscope but the man was still sitting there. He was an older man and there was something strangely familiar about him. He just kept sitting there, staring at the water as if he owned the place. So we waited, and waited, and waited, hoping he would leave. But he never did. Finally, he stood up and stared at the water really closely. Then I saw a brown shadow pass in front of the periscope. Oh no! Seaweed was standing on it! The man was sure to notice that.

He did! Shoot! Now we had to go find another cove. And now somebody had spotted us and would report us. Rats! Unless . . . what if we made friends with him? Maybe he wouldn't tell anybody about us. Usually when people realized we were not a threat they were pretty friendly. We had nothing to lose.

He was standing on the edge of the rock, shielding his eyes from the sun when we surfaced. His hands dropped and his mouth fell open. But I had seen him before somewhere. Who was he?

I opened the hatch and sure enough, Seaweed was standing there, waiting for breakfast. I pulled a handful of dog biscuits from my pocket and threw them to him. That must have looked pretty strange to the man on the beach. I waved. The man slowly raised his hand and waved back. I reached in, pulled out the Spanish flag and hung it from the portal. He hollered out to me something in Spanish but I didn't understand. He made a sweeping gesture with his arms for us to come closer. So we did. I motored over until we were just fifty feet away. Now I knew who he was. He was Douglas Nickels, Ziegfried's favourite movie star!

He said something in Spanish.

"I'm sorry, I don't speak . . ."

"You're English!" he barked.

"I'm Canadian."

"Canadian?"

"Yes."

"Are you a photographer?"

"No, I'm an explorer."

"An explorer?"

"Yes."

"Are you sure you aren't here to take pictures?"

"No, I'm here to see the goats."

"The goats?"

"Yes."

"What goats?"

"The mountain goats."

He looked confused. I wondered if I was on the right island.

"Oh! Yes. The goats up in the hills. You came here to see *them*?"

"Yes."

"What's your name?"

"Alfred."

"And you're from Canada?"

"Yes."

"How old are you?"

"Fifteen."

He stopped and thought for a while. I waited to see what he would do.

"Did you just feed that seagull?"

"Yes. That's Seaweed. He's part of the crew."

"Oh. Is there anyone else?"

"Just Hollie," I said, and climbed down, grabbed Hollie and carried him up.

Douglas Nickels nodded, then made a sweeping gesture with his arms and said, "Come over, Alfred. I'd like to meet you."

So I moored to the rock and climbed out with Hollie. There was a small, pebbled beach in the center of the cove. It was very private. Hollie was delighted. Mr. Nickels greeted me with a strong handshake.

"Call me Doug," he said.

"I'm Alfred."

"I'm very pleased to meet you, Alfred. Welcome to my little beach."

"Is it really yours? Do you *own* it?"

"Yes, I do. Our house is up there. My wife, Greta Sachs, is there. Do you know her?"

"I think I've heard of her, but I'm not sure what she looks like."

He laughed. "You're not sure what Greta Sachs looks like? But you know she's a movie star, right?"

"I guess so."

"Hah! That's great! You'll have to come up for a cup of tea, Alfred. Come on up."

"I don't want to bother you."

"Nonsense! You're a breath of fresh air. And you've got to meet Greta. She won't believe this."

Doug and Greta lived in the biggest house I had ever seen. It stretched over the rock in all directions and I could easily have gotten lost inside of it. It made me think of the maze at King Minos' palace that I was hoping to see on Crete. The house was very, very fancy and yet Doug walked through it in his wet, sandy sneakers as if it were a boathouse. Except for his famous face, you wouldn't have known him from any other fisherman on the sea.

I didn't see anyone else in the house until we entered a room where Greta Sachs was sitting on a sofa, reading a book. I immediately recognized her, though, like Doug, she looked a lot older in real life.

"Dougie?" she said, without looking up.

"Greta, I'd like you to meet someone."

"Dougie? . . . Oh! . . . Hello."

"Hi."

"Greta. This is Alfred."

"Hello, Alfred. How are you?"

"Fine, thank you."

"Alfred is a young explorer, Greta. He has come all the way from Canada."

"Oh. That's nice. What are you looking for, Alfred?"

"Ummm . . . Atlantis."

"Oh, that's nice. I hope you find it. Dougie?"

"Yes?"

"We've got ants."

"Really? Oh. Well, I'll get Francis to call the exterminators in the morning. Greta, Alfred is travelling in a submarine."

"Francis is off tomorrow."

"Oh, that's right. Well, I'll just have to get some ant traps myself then. Alfred here is travelling in his very own submarine. He has come to Mallorca to see the mountain goats."

Greta raised her head, took a closer look at me and smiled. "You must be very brave, Alfred."

"He is indeed," said Doug. "I've got half a mind to join you tomorrow, Alfred. What do you say, could you stand a little company on your mountain trek?"

"Ummm . . . I guess so."

"Splendid! We'll have an adventure."

Greta smiled and lowered her head. "Don't forget the ant traps, Dougie."

Chapter Nineteen

❦

I COULDN'T BELIEVE IT.

First, Doug decided he didn't have a suitable pair of hiking boots, or any proper hiking equipment. When I suggested he just wear his sneakers, like me, he said, no, he might sprain an ankle. We went to see Greta, who was up early and running on a treadmill. She looked very fit. She advised that we carry adequate water and salt tablets, to avoid heat exhaustion. Don't forget a first-aid kit too, she said. And don't forget the ant traps.

It was only a hike. But Doug concluded that we'd have to make a trip into the city first, to a hiking shop, where we could get properly outfitted. The drive would bring us closer to the trails into the hills anyway, he said. So, we climbed into his fancy jeep, buckled up and headed for the city.

It was a nice drive. We sped through the countryside, which was very beautiful. There were little towns with old houses and churches, and monasteries on hilltops here and there, just like in books. Doug put on a baseball cap and sunglasses when we left the house, and gave me the same to wear, so that we would look just like any two Joes, he said. I put them on and smiled. I felt a little bit like a movie star.

After an hour or so we reached the city, which looked pretty fancy, with beautiful old buildings and an enormous cathedral by the water. Doug pointed out lots of things, including a giant yacht in the harbour, which belonged to him. He said he would like to show me around the city some time. Hanging out with him like that made me forget that he was a famous person. The moment we stepped out of the jeep and entered the hiking shop . . . that all changed.

You would have thought he was the king. When we entered the shop and he removed his hat and glasses, the shopkeepers flocked to us, asking how they could help. Doug told them what we were planning to do and what he thought we might need. In a flash they disappeared and reappeared with boxes and armloads of boots, backpacks, climbing rope, tents, sleeping bags, dried food, cooking utensils, gas stoves, and so on. One employee even carried over a small kayak. I couldn't believe it. After an hour or so, we were both standing in brand new hiking clothes — boots, hats, watches . . .

the whole shebang. We each had a new backpack filled with dried food, medical kits, anti-dehydration drinks, spare socks, and many, many things which I couldn't ever imagine using. Doug insisted on buying pretty much everything they offered. We piled the stuff into the back of the jeep, waved goodbye to the admiring shopkeepers and drove away.

"Whew!" said Doug. "All that shopping made me hungry. What do you say we stop for a bite to eat first? I know a nice little restaurant nearby."

It didn't surprise me that the nice little restaurant was really fancy, nor that the waiters made a fuss over us, but I was concerned with the sign on the door that showed a picture of a dog crossed out.

"What does that mean?" I asked.

Doug translated the sign. "Absolutely NO dogs allowed in the restaurant!" he said.

"Oh. Well . . . maybe Hollie and I can wait . . ."

"No, no, it doesn't mean us," said Doug.

He was right. The waiters treated Hollie just like any other customer and even set a place for him at the table, although I insisted he stay on the floor. So they brought him a plate of sausages and finely cut meats and laid it down on the floor in front of him, with a napkin. Then one waiter opened a bottle of spring water, filled a bowl with it, set the bowl down on the floor beside the plate, and stood there and waited while Hollie ate.

The breakfast was amazing. I ate way too much, and it made me sleepy (it was my bedtime anyway). The new clothes were making me a little itchy but I was almost too sleepy to scratch. I looked down at Hollie and saw that he was sleepy too. Then Doug insisted I try their coffee. So I did. After I put a couple of spoonfuls of sugar in the cup, the coffee tasted pretty good. And so I had another cup. Then another. I had no idea what I was in for. By the time we left the restaurant, I was ready to run circles around Hollie all the way up the mountain.

It was almost noon when we parked the jeep at the top of a hill, where the road came to an end and a narrow trail disappeared into some dry bushes, rocks and trees. There was a loud, high-pitched sound in the air, like a soft siren, coming from the tops of trees and echoing everywhere. It was strangely pleasant. It made me think of the desert, though I didn't know why, except that I really wanted to see the desert. Doug said it was the singing of tree frogs. Then, when we stepped out of the air-conditioned jeep, I realized for the first time — it was scorching hot! With our new itchy clothes, new boots and heavy packs, we were in for a tough hike.

But it was a dry heat, which was not so bad, especially as our new wide-brimmed hats kept the sun off our faces. I wished I could have put a hat on Hollie, because he had no protection at all, although he cleverly walked in our shadows. Every time we stopped to drink our special anti-dehydration drinks, I gave him some water.

But we didn't see any goats. I kept looking for them and watching Hollie for any sign that he smelled them, but the trail was steep and the hike so much work for him he barely had a chance to sniff. I had read that you would smell the goats before you would see them, and so I kept sniffing the air for them, but smelled only our new clothes.

After a couple of hours of climbing we sat down to rest. Doug searched through his pack.

"I didn't remember how beautiful it was from up here. What's this?" he said, as he pulled out a strange looking tool.

It was shaped like a spoon with a lot of holes. I stared at it and tried to remember.

"Ummm . . . maybe it's a sieve? I'm not sure."

"Well . . . I suppose we should cook something. Here's a nice looking soup."

We dug out the little gas stove, poured the soup contents into a pot and filled it with water. Doug checked his pockets.

"Hey, Alfred, do you have any matches?"

"No."

"Me either. Shoot!"

It didn't matter; there was no gas in the stove anyway.

Three hours later, we reached the top. The view was absolutely amazing, but there were no goats. We were so tired we just flopped down and didn't move for about fifteen minutes. Then, slowly, we raised our heads, drank more anti-dehydration liquid and licked at our dry soups. Hollie was sleeping. I figured I'd have to carry him down the mountain. I looked over at Doug, licking his soup and looking tired and kind of thoughtful.

"Doug?"

"Yah?"

"Do you believe in Atlantis?"

"Atlantis? Sure. Why not? I don't think it's a city under a bubble somewhere, like some people think. But there are lots of temples under water. I have seen some myself. There are cities under sand too, even whole pyramids. And I've seen ancient temples swallowed up by jungle in Central America. We shot some movies there."

"Cool."

"So . . . yes, I think it exists . . . *somewhere*. And you're probably headed in the right direction."

"I hope so."

I stared out to sea. It always fascinated me to see the water from such a height. You could see the curvature of the earth. It made the world seem smaller.

"Why do you suppose that nobody's found Atlantis before?"

Doug shrugged. "I don't know. Maybe because of expectations."

"Expectations?"

"Well, if you are expecting to find a city under a bubble, you're not going to pay much attention to one that isn't."

"Oh." That was a good point.

"But promise me something, Alfred?"

"What?"

"If you do find a city under a bubble, come and tell me before the whole world sees it, okay? I'd like to see it first. Okay?"

I laughed. "Okay."

"Good. Actually, I'm glad to know that *somebody* is looking for Atlantis. Now, I suppose we should get our carcasses back down the mountain. You know what we forgot to buy?"

"What?"

"Ant traps."

The moment we stood up and started down the mountain I picked up a strong smell; it was like being inside a barn full of stinky animals. Hollie rode in my backpack and stuck his nose out stiffly and made his quietest growl, which always sounded like a tiny electric motor. But we had only the smell — no goats.

There were crevices here and there, and sharp jagged cliffs, but they were not places where any creature could climb, not even mountain goats. Or so I thought. The smell was so strong towards the cliff, I just had to lie down, crawl to the edge and peek over. As I inched my eyes over the very edge of the cliff and nervously peeked down, which was a dizzying experience, I saw surprised faces looking up at me, whiskered faces, with goatee beards and curled horns. How they could be standing there I just could not understand.

The goats were not happy about having been discovered and started to move. I wished they wouldn't because I was sure they were going to fall, and I felt terrible about it. It would be my fault because I had scared them. Well, miraculously, they didn't fall. Neither did they fall when they scurried across another impossible precipice and up an even steeper cliff. Like big fat birds with long skinny legs, the goats disappeared. Their smell lingered though, and so did my amazement.

It was dark when we returned to the jeep. We were exhausted and starving. I was dying for pizza. Doug said he knew the best place. So we drove there. But the employees and customers made such a fuss over Doug we couldn't seem to place our order. Finally we went somewhere else. This time, Doug waited in the jeep while I went in and ordered. I was beginning to see how difficult the life of a famous person could be. It was sort of like being an outlaw.

We stuffed our faces and drove back to the cove where Hollie and I returned to the sub to sleep. The next day Doug met us on the beach with a big smile. He was holding up one of the local newspapers. On the front page was a picture of the two of us coming out of the hiking shop in our ball caps and sunglasses. The headline read:

IS THIS DOUGLAS NICKELS' ILLEGITIMATE SON?

Later, as we climbed into the dinghy to leave, Doug shook my hand firmly and asked me to promise to visit on our way back home. I promised. I was beginning to understand something Sheba had told me. She said it was the interesting places that made you travel somewhere, but the people that made you go back. How true.

Chapter Twenty

"DID YOU GET HIS autograph, Al?"

"Uh . . . no, I never thought about it."

"You spent a couple of days with Douglas Nickels and didn't even get his autograph?"

"He's just a regular guy. . . well, except out in public. You wouldn't believe the fuss people make over him."

"I think I would. Do you realize he's married to Greta Sachs, one of the most beautiful women in the world?"

"Sheba's more beautiful!"

"Al. Are you telling me you met Greta Sachs too?"

"Yes, but Sheba's more beautiful and a *lot* smarter."

"I will tell her you said that. But Geez, Al, what did Greta Sachs say?"

"Not much. She really wanted some ant traps but we forgot to buy them."

"Unbelievable! So what's next? Where are you sailing next?"

"Well, I think I should avoid France, because they've got the biggest submarine fleet in the Mediterranean. I think we'll go south from here, towards Italy."

"I'm looking at the map as we speak. Looks like Corsica and Sardinia are in your path."

"I know but we can sail between them, through the Strait of Bonifacio."

"Italy has submarines too, you know."

"Oh yah. Well, maybe I should stick to North Africa. It's pretty nice there and it's a lot less busy."

"Okay, but avoid Libya. The newspapers say there are terrorists there."

"I will, though I don't believe everything the newspapers say."

"Better safe than sorry, Al."

"True."

Ziegfried was the voice of caution.

I decided to sail for Tunisia for a chance to peek at the greatest desert in the world. It would have been nice to sail through the Strait of Bonifacio, but that was just too risky.

The north side was Corsica, a large island belonging to France, and the birthplace of Napoleon. The south side was Sardinia, a large island belonging to Italy. Both would have been patrolled by navy and coastguard ships, possibly even submarines. In fact, according to my guidebooks, there were twenty-four NATO bases on Sardinia. Yikes! But Sardinia also had a few incredible things, such as a herd of miniature horses and the world's only albino donkeys. The miniature horses really were horses, not ponies, even though they stood only three feet tall. How I wished I could have seen them. But they were too far inland. I didn't see how we could get there.

The problem with the donkeys was that they were on a smaller island, Isola Asinara, that also just happened to have a maximum-security prison. It was little wonder I had a bad feeling about that place.

Something else Sardinia was famous for was its caves. They were cut out of cliffs that dropped into the sea. Since we were going to sail so close to the island anyway, I thought maybe we could take a peek at the cliffs as we went by, maybe even get Hollie out for a run on the beach.

From a distance, through binoculars, the caves looked like black dots on a white birthday cake. I entered the twelve-mile zone a bit nervously. Why would one island have twenty-four NATO bases anyway? Canada was part of NATO, the North Atlantic Treaty Organization, and maybe that would work in our favour if we were stopped. We crossed the line before dawn and I raised the Canadian and Italian flags while it was still dark, just in case we were being watched as the sun came up.

Five miles from the cliffs I hadn't picked up much on radar, just a few fishing boats. For an island with twenty-four NATO bases it seemed strangely quiet. And then, from the north came a radar beep, and it was coming in too fast to be a ship. Yikes! A helicopter or a plane! We didn't even have time to dive. Well, we could have dived but would have been spotted from the air anyway, the very moment we appeared on their radar screen. It was a good thing we were not submerged, and were sailing with proper flags. We were at least legal.

It was a small plane. It flew right over our heads, made a turn and a second pass, taking a closer look. I stood on the portal and waved. I wanted to show them we were friendly. The plane dipped its wing, a way of saying hello. That was a good sign. They must have identified our flags. Was it the coastguard? I couldn't tell. Maybe it was just a pleasure craft. Would they report us? Probably, but I couldn't know for sure. What to do — take the chance and go see the caves, or play it cautious and leave the twelve-mile zone? What would Ziegfried do? I looked down the portal at Hollie, wagging his tail and staring up expectantly. "I'm sorry, Hollie. There will be other beaches. We'll find another one." I turned the sub around. Less than an hour later I was glad I did. Radar revealed two ships leaving the shore in our direction, but too far away to catch us before we reached the twelve-mile zone. Then, just as we were leaving the zone, the plane flew over us once again. This time I got a closer look at it with binoculars. It was the Italian coastguard all right. I waved again as we left their waters. They dipped their wing. Ciao!

We would have to visit caves somewhere else.

Tunisia offered the best opportunity to see the Sahara. The desert wore a collar of mountains along its northern border, hundreds of miles thick in places. But in Tunisia, in the Gulf of Gabes, the Sahara reached up a thin finger and touched the sea. It was the one spot where we had a chance to see it, if we were lucky.

Also in the Gulf of Gabes was the island of Jerba, where fishermen still dived for sea sponges, although it was a dying tradition. And, there were reports of a sunken city! Could it be Atlantis? Probably not.

Gabes, a coastal town on the mainland, was the gateway to Chott El Jerid, a large salt lake that supposedly sparkled like jewels but was as barren as the moon. It was a place where you could see mirages. I wanted to see that too!

It took only a day to reach the coast of Tunisia. In the Atlantic, a day's journey didn't take you very far. In the Mediterranean it took you everywhere. But we were now two days at sea without a break. I hadn't slept at all, and Hollie hadn't been out for a run. The coast of Tunisia made a sudden downward turn, like an elbow joint, and went south for about six hundred miles before straightening out on the border with Libya. In the darkness of night, with our lights on and a hot breeze coming from the desert, we went down the coast, keeping an eye open for traffic and ready to flee at the first sign of trouble. Just a couple of hours before sunrise we reached the island of Jerba, the Land of the Lotus-Eaters, according to my guidebook, and the very island where Odysseus and his crew were bewitched into never wanting to leave. As beautiful as it might be, I didn't think we would have that problem.

The periscope revealed a makeshift breakwater — just a pile of large rocks tossed into the sea — a wide beach, and not a soul. I surfaced and opened the hatch. Seaweed went out and inspected our surroundings. Hollie and I climbed out, moored the sub to a rock and hopped onto the beach.

Hollie was such a smart dog. He never barked in a strange place. Nor did he run far away. We went down the beach about half a mile, back up, and down again. The air was hot and dry and very pleasant. The sand was warm beneath my feet. The sky sparkled like a chest full of jewels. It felt wonderful to be back on the continent of Africa.

Chapter Twenty-One

SOMETIMES YOU MEET someone, and know right away you
will become good friends.

I slept through the entire day and most of the night. I
brought the sub up a few hours before sunrise, opened the
hatch, tossed Seaweed some dog biscuits and took Hollie
out for another run on the beach. This time, I moored the
sub between rocks at the breakwater and left it awash, the
bow and stern submerged, just half of the portal sticking out
of the water. When we returned from our walk I made a
proper breakfast and we sat on the hatch and watched the
sun come up. Hollie was happy. The life of a submariner was
sometimes peaceful beyond words.

When I felt confident we were well enough hidden, I brought Hollie back inside, put the radio on for him, gave him a new ball, went out and shut the hatch. I intended to practise diving here, where divers supposedly brought up sponges from the bottom and my guidebook said there were rumours of a sunken city.

In the three years since I had met Ziegfried and we began to build the sub, I had learned to free-dive to nearly a hundred feet and hold my breath for two minutes. It didn't seem like such a big deal now but there was a time when forty-five seconds and forty feet were way beyond my reach. Improving on that had taken me a *lot* of practice.

The water beneath the sub was only seventy-five feet, so I swam out a little ways, to where I guessed it was ninety feet, did my breathing exercises and went down. The sea was as warm as a bathtub. The early morning sun pierced the water for about thirty feet or so. Compared to the dark water back home, it was like another planet.

It was easier to dive more deeply and hold my breath longer in warmer water, and this made diving more fun. I was having such a good time in fact that I just kind of assumed I was alone in the water.

I wasn't.

At the bottom I discovered sponges attached to rocks, just like the sponges Sheba kept in her bathroom back in Newfoundland, except maybe a little rougher. I put my hand on one and squeezed it. It felt the same, but was attached to the rock and wouldn't come off with a strong tug. It would have to be cut off. I decided to return to the sub for a knife. I turned . . . and froze! No more than fifteen feet away was a large shark! It came straight towards me then veered off at the last second. Its mouth was open and I saw rows of jagged teeth. It all happened so quickly I never had time to think. I was frightened but didn't panic. The shark swam around in a circle then came back. It was fast! I had to return to the surface for air but was afraid to move. The shark came towards me again so quickly I saw its whole body shake with exertion. I got ready to duck. Just then, a slim brown body went over my head, straight towards the shark! The shark veered again and vanished. The figure was holding a knife in his hand. He turned and faced me. He smiled.

We swam to the surface. I saw that he had a floating burlap bag he was filling with sponges. The bag was tied to three plastic jugs, which acted as a buoy. He didn't have a boat; he had swum out from the beach all by himself. He was pretty excited to have found me and said something in an excited voice that I didn't understand. Then, he gestured that we should dive again. Wasn't he afraid of the shark, I gestured? He shrugged, not at all! He started breathing exercises, just the way I did them. So . . . I joined him.

Together we went down and I watched as he expertly cut sponges from the rock and put them in a smaller bag. He worked quickly but calmly. I kept watch for sharks.

His name was Omar. He was my age and my height. He was very lean and in amazing shape. We made about ten dives together, which was great practice for me. I saw two more sharks but they didn't bother us. I could tell Omar did a lot of diving the way he moved so gracefully in the water. Beside him I felt rather clumsy. He let me hold the knife a couple of times and showed me how to cut the sponges free. I chose two nice ones to bring back for Sheba.

When Omar's bag was filled, we swam towards shore. I pointed in the direction of the sub, which we couldn't really see from where we were. He wore a questioning look on his face. I said, "submarine," but that didn't help. I started to swim towards the sub and gestured for him to follow me. I would just have to show him.

Omar was fearless against sharks but absolutely frightened of the submarine. He stared at it as if it were a sea monster and wouldn't come close to it at all. I tried to coax him but he shook his head. So, I climbed up, opened the hatch, went inside and brought out Hollie. When he saw Hollie, he broke into a big smile and started to relax. Eventually he came over and climbed up, but would not come inside.

Later, we sat on the beach and communicated by drawing pictures in the sand. Seaweed dropped by when he saw us scratching with a stick, and so, the first thing I had to explain was that Seaweed was part of the crew. That wasn't easy. Then Omar explained that he was from the desert. As far as I could tell from his sand pictures, he sometimes travelled through the desert by camel, with his family, and sometimes came sponge diving, all by himself. That was his favourite thing to do; I could tell by the way he smiled when he drew himself diving. But he missed his family then. I asked him how many brothers and sisters he had. He drew twelve figures in the sand. Wow. Beside his father he drew three women. Did his father have three sisters, I asked? No. Three wives. Oh.

From another picture Omar drew, it looked as though they also had a farm in the desert. I couldn't understand how anyone could have a farm in the desert, but he drew a picture of a mountain, and put the farm on the side of it. Then he drew rain clouds and scratched them out. There wasn't enough water? He nodded.

The hardest thing for Omar to understand was the submarine. Why didn't it sink? The only way I could really show him that was to coax him inside. That took a long time. He came down the ladder as cautiously as a cat and looked around with wide eyes. He caught sight of the pellet rifles and nodded his head approvingly. I picked one up and gave it to him. That made him so happy he hugged me. Then I showed him the engine compartment and the piles of toys still wrapped in their plastic packages. Would his brothers and sisters like these things, I asked? Yes, indeed. But when Omar saw the engine, his mouth dropped and his eyes grew very serious. He tried to explain something to me, something very important, but he was gesturing too fast and I couldn't understand. I gave him a piece of paper and pencil and he very carefully drew a long diagram. When he handed me the paper, I stared at the picture and tried to figure out what it all meant. He kept pointing to the engine and the diagram on the paper, which included a map. Was there another engine? Yes. Did he want me to see it? Yes. Did he want me to *fix* it? Yes. Was it far away? Not too far, he said, three or four days by camel. Would I come, he asked? Yes I would!

But I did have a few concerns. Where would I hide the sub for so long? Three or four days out meant three or four days back. I would also probably need a few days to work on the engine, maybe more. That meant at least a week and a half. I could take Hollie with me, for sure, but what would I do with Seaweed? I didn't mind leaving him for a couple of days, but nine or ten days was too long. Could a seagull survive in the desert if he had enough water? I would have to ask Ziegfried. I needed to consult with him about fixing the engine anyway. Which tools should I bring? Which spare parts? Although he had taught me many things in the last three years, I was still only an apprentice when it came to engines.

We took the pellet rifles over to the beach, set up targets and practised shooting for hours. When we ran out of pellets we combed the beach for tiny round pebbles that fit in the rifles. It was the most fun I had had in the longest time. I asked Omar if anyone might discover us. Should I worry about my passport? He said, no, nobody would come. And when we went into the desert, I would wear a cloth around my head, just like him, and no one would know me. Cool.

Chapter Twenty-two

"WHAT'S THE SITUATION?"

"I'm pretty sure it's a diesel engine. They use it for pumping water uphill to irrigate their fields."

"I see."

Ziegfried was quiet for a while. I could picture his face. He was adding up things in his mind. His mind was like a computer, accurate and thorough. It was always beyond me.

"Chances are it's a very old engine. If it is, there's not a lot you can take apart, which is a good thing. Perhaps something's interfering with the fuel injection, or the oil, or both. Keep in mind, all an engine sometimes needs is just a really good tune up and a really good cleaning. People add oil to their engines endlessly, never thinking to change it. So, you'll want to bring fresh oil with you. Bring enough to soak the engine. Drain it, fill it, run it, drain it . . . and fill it again. Take the head off, and you'll probably want to flush the cylinders with diesel. Clean the engine first, flush it, dry it and feed it new oil. Clean the oil and air filters. Then you'll have a better idea what might be wrong with it, other than any obvious visual defects. Bring all your universal hoses, adaptors, wire, bolts, the whole shebang, plus your tools, of course. Don't forget your files. Keep a list and I'll bring replacements for anything you leave behind."

"Okay. What about Seaweed?"

"He should be fine, I think, but you'll want to soak all his food in water. Watch out for snakes, though. Birds and snakes are mortal enemies. And watch out for yourself, Al. Snakes, spiders, scorpions . . . the desert sun . . . Holy Smokes, are you sure you want to go?"

"Yes, I'm sure."

"Okay. But keep my little buddy real close to you. I don't want to hear about him getting stepped on by a camel or bitten by a snake."

"Will do."

Ziegfried meant Hollie, of course. He had a soft spot for all birds and animals, but especially for Hollie, because Hollie was such a runt, although he was probably the smartest runt that ever stood on four legs.

After studying the maps, Omar and I discovered that if we met up on the coast just north of Gabes, he on camel, me in the sub, we could shorten our trek to the foothills of Jebel Biada, the mountain where the pump engine was. Just two days by camel would be enough to get us there, he said. I had to take his word on that, having never actually seen a real camel myself, or a desert. I asked him if we would see the salt lakes on our way, but try as I might I couldn't get him to understand what I meant.

It would take two days for him to meet me. That was fine. That gave me time to explore the bay for the sunken city and to find a suitable place to hide the sub. Omar told me to watch out for sharks and to be tough with them. Treat them like wild dogs, he said. Kick at them, rush at them, never let them think you are afraid of them. Okay, I said. I asked if he knew anything about the sunken city. He shook his head, but I didn't think he really understood what I was asking, and I was too tired to explain.

He left with his sack of sponges, which now included a pellet rifle and a whole bunch of toys. He would sell the sponges in the market, walk across the island about five miles, take the ferry to the mainland and walk another fifteen miles to get home! Once there, he would explain everything to his father and prepare the camels to meet me. We shook hands warmly; he hugged me and went on his way. I watched him disappear down the beach, the long sack hanging over his shoulder.

I climbed into the sub, sleepy now, but determined to turn my sleep around for the week. I didn't want to be falling asleep when we were riding camels. The radar showed no traffic so I submerged and went out into the bay, keeping just twenty feet or so above the bottom so that I could look down through the observation window. I coaxed Seaweed in with a snack, because he was such a good scout at the window. But three hours of zigzagging around the bay revealed nothing but old urns, broken pottery, and a few wooden boat skeletons. I realized now that there wasn't just the sand of the sea to contend with, there were thousands of years of sand blowing from the land and settling into the sea that could hide a sunken city just as easily as a land city. Atlantis might be a lot harder to find than I thought.

Hollie never showed any interest in the observation window because he couldn't smell anything. Seaweed gazed diligently with a patience only a seagull could muster. But after three hours he hadn't tapped on the glass even once. Okay then. I settled on the bottom and went to sleep.

We planned to meet north of Gabes, on the beach where an old freighter had run aground. I didn't remember seeing one, but Omar insisted it was there. He said he would light a fire on the beach at night and that is how I should find him. I had no trouble finding the old ship. It was a Greek, steel-hulled freighter, rusted to a reddish brown, deck and cabin included. The ship had run aground on the sandbar ages ago and lay on her side about a hundred feet from shore. The problem was, I couldn't find any suitable place to moor the sub, especially to keep it out of sight for a whole week. Back and forth I cruised along the coast, looking for a sheltered cove, but it just wasn't that kind of shoreline. It was all open and exposed. Finally, I stumbled upon the most obvious idea — why not moor the sub to the freighter itself? If I left it awash, with the portal sticking up just a couple of inches, and moored it on the seaward side, no one would ever notice it.

Then I found something even better. Pulling up alongside the stranded ship, I climbed out and jumped onto it. After a bit of exploring, I discovered part of the bridge was submerged and part exposed, with a covered roof. Would it be possible to tuck the sub right in beneath where the bridge was on its side, such that the portal came up through a window into the cabin? Then it would be hidden from the beach and the sky as well. The only way anyone would discover it would be if they climbed onto the old ship and looked inside, into its murky interior. What were the chances of that?

But motoring the sub underneath the crooked old ship wasn't easy. There were so many odd surfaces to bounce sonar waves off I wasn't sure what I was seeing on the screen. Several times the sub gently bumped against the rusty metal and made a terrible squealing sound, like a wailing pig. I wasn't too worried about the ship shifting its position; it probably hadn't moved in thirty years, but I was a little concerned about getting stuck. I had to go completely under the surface to get the portal inside the bridge. Once inside, I carefully surfaced until the portal was about a foot out of the water. It was dark and kind of creepy. I would wait until the sun came up and review the situation.

It was another whole day before Omar would arrive. I decided to spend the morning organizing parts and tools, and a week's supply of food for the crew. In the afternoon I would practise diving, the afternoon being when sharks were least likely to be feeding. I would take a nap before dark.

It turned out to be a good idea to spend a day at the ship. It gave Seaweed a chance to get used to it. There were lots of little crabs and various things to keep a seagull busy should he return before us. That's what I was most afraid of, that he'd return, not see us for a few days and wander off. So long as he could see the sub, he ought to assume we would eventually return, as always. I just didn't know how long he would wait. I would leave an old shirt of mine on top of the hatch, just to help prod his memory. Seagulls, I knew, were the ultimate masters of survival. And Seaweed was remarkable among seagulls. Still, I would worry about him.

In the tail end of twilight I saw four camels walk onto the beach. What strange looking creatures they were. Their movement was odd too, at least from a distance, and in the growing darkness. I climbed into the sub, took out the dinghy and inflated it, but left Hollie behind, because I didn't know how he would take to the camels and didn't want to lose him in the dark if he ran away.

Omar had a fire burning by the time I reached the beach. But he was not alone. He had brought his father and uncle.

Chapter Twenty-three

THE CAMELS HATED Hollie. On top of that, they were terrified of him. It was the strangest of meetings — four large, bad-tempered camels and one little dog. Hollie dominated them and intimidated them from the start. I wondered if it were partly because they never really got a good look at him. But I had to hide him from them or we would never have gotten him onto their backs and on our way. I had to wrap him up in a scarf and lift him onto the camel's back in a woven bag. And that's where he remained most of the time, making his little belly-growl on and off for the first couple of hours, which the camels couldn't hear, fortunately, although they seemed to suspect he was there because they would occasionally look back nervously. But the camel drivers — Omar, his father and uncle — were strict with the desert beasts. They made it very clear from the beginning: the camels were not pets.

Omar didn't look anything like his father or uncle. I even wondered if he might have been adopted. Either that or the desert sun had aged the older men before their time, because they were as wrinkled as dried-out potatoes, like my grandfather, whereas Omar's skin was as smooth as an apple.

The men greeted me loudly with words, which I was pretty certain were blessings, took my hands in theirs and hugged me. Then, when they saw the sack of tools I was carrying, they nodded their heads respectfully. I had to admit I was feeling pretty important.

That feeling of importance diminished quite a bit the first time I fell off the camel. It was just the irregular movement of the beast; I failed to get into rhythm with it. The second time I fell, my feeling of importance left entirely. It was a long way to the ground and it really hurt. It wasn't going to happen a third time. Hollie, fortunately, had better balance than I did. I tried to make myself feel better by telling Omar that I had spent so much time at sea, my land balance was rusty. He smiled and nodded his head sympathetically, which was kind because I knew he didn't have a clue what I was talking about.

The camels were pretty stinky and definitely bad tempered but it was still fun riding them. I was surprised how slow it was, but it might only have appeared slow because of the extreme wide-open spaces. When we left the beach and crossed a small rise in the land, the desert opened up endlessly and just sort of vanished into a haze on the horizon. Once we were away from the water, the temperature rose at least ten degrees, very suddenly. Omar gave me a white *dishdasha* (a long gown) to wear over my t-shirt and shorts, and helped me wrap a blue cloth around my head, leaving only a slit open for my nose and eyes. This protected me from the hot sun and kept me cooler. I wished I had brought a mirror and camera.

Two hours into the trek I was already terribly sleepy. The movement of the camel, bobbing and weaving like a poorly built dory, had such a slow steadiness to it, which, combined with the intense heat and absolute stillness, was like a sleeping potion. The barren landscape, that was fascinating to look at for the first hour or so, gradually began to remind me of the sea, except that the sea would keep me awake because it was always moving.

We reached Chott el Fedjaj, one of the salt lakes. It was a salt lake all right; there wasn't even any water! Only salt! I thought they should have called it a salt *field*. But they could have called it a crystal lake too, because in places it sparkled like crystals. It did something else. After an hour moving across the lake I spotted a very long camel caravan on the far horizon, passing in the opposite direction. I called out to Omar to look at it, but he didn't see it. "Look!" I shouted.

"Look at all the camels!" There must have been hundreds of them in a straight line, loaded up with all kinds of strange packages. Then, when I looked again, they were gone. They were never there. That was my first, and best, mirage.

By the afternoon, Seaweed, who had been following in the sky mostly, after an unsuccessful attempt to get comfortable on a camel's back, headed back to the sea. I watched him spiral upwards, slowly, until he reached the highest level I had ever seen him reach. I knew he was looking for the sea. When he saw it he straightened out and sailed towards it. I had mixed feelings watching him go. Probably it was for the best. He would find the rusty old ship and the submarine, and would hang out there until I returned. But now I was more aware of the time. I would work on the engine as soon as we arrived, and wouldn't stop until I was done.

We spent one night in the desert, which was unbelievably cold! Maybe it was the contrast with the day, I didn't know, but the desert sand didn't retain heat at night the way beach sand did. I slept with my clothes on, wrapped up in my sleeping bag, Hollie on my feet. The nice part of it was that, once we had set up the tent, which was a long, sloping, black cloth tent, and made a fire, and eaten, Omar's father and uncle started playing music. They brought out a stringed instrument, something like a small round guitar, and a wooden flute set in a stone-like gourd. When they started to play, I recognized the sound instantly. I had heard this kind of music on the radio. Omar and I kept the beat by hitting sticks together. But I couldn't keep my eyes open for long and was the first one to crawl into the tent. I didn't even remember falling asleep. Crossing a desert by camel was completely exhausting. The heat just sucked all the energy out of you.

On the morning of the second day we could already see the mountain we were aiming towards. Under the burning sun the mountain sometimes looked twice its height, and sometimes disappeared altogether! It was unbelievable. We tossed and pitched in a straight line towards it like ants crossing a beach. As morning passed into afternoon, and afternoon dragged into evening, I fell into a kind of hypnotic state, a bit like sleepwalking. The desert wasn't a place to be alone with your thoughts; it was a place to lose your thoughts and just listen to your breath. I thought Sheba would have liked it; it reminded me of how she described her yoga exercises. Personally, I would be happy to get back to my submarine.

It was dark when we got in. I couldn't even remember the last couple of hours on the camel. I plopped down on my sleeping bag as soon as the tent was set up and fell asleep instantly. When I got up in the morning, I saw that we had reached the foot of the mountain. Strangely, the mountain started as abruptly as if someone had simply drawn a line in the sand and said, "Okay, here's where we'll put the mountain."

There was a small wooden shack with pipes running out

of it. The pipes snaked up the sides of the mountain. The mountain itself looked too dry for growing anything, but Omar insisted that it did. Inside the shack I found the engine. It was indeed an ancient two-cylinder diesel. Someone had hooked it up rather cleverly to a pump to drive water up the mountain from a deep well. As I looked around the interior of the shack, I saw thin slits of golden light pushing in through cracks between the wooden boards. If the sun was coming in, then so was the fine desert sand that floated on the air with the slightest breeze and found its way inside everything. Sealing those cracks was something they would have to do. Sand was the enemy of an engine.

I carried in my tools and set to work. Hollie dropped into a corner with his ball. He was happy to be out of the sun and off the back of the camel.

First, I sprayed anti-rust fluid on the engine bolts that hadn't been removed in ages, and let it sit to loosen them up. Then I removed the bolts with a wrench, following the reverse of the pattern that had been stamped onto the head of the engine, many years before I was born. Although the engine itself wasn't all that big — about half as big as a desk — I needed Omar's help to lift off the head. Inside, I found the pistons covered with a very thin layer of fine, clay-like muck, which must have been a mixture of desert powder and engine oil. Whatever it was, it was *not* good for an engine. The muck was everywhere.

But the real shock came when I drained the engine oil. I

knew it hadn't been changed for a very long time because the drain cap was so hard to get off. I had to spray it, let it sit and pry it with vice-grips. Ziegfried was right, whoever had been looking after the engine had merely added new oil. My grandfather was a bit like that too. Oil was oil, he used to say, it turns black the second it goes into an engine, why waste money on new oil? My grandfather thought that when his boat engine coughed and hiccuped, it was supposed to sound like that.

I watched the filthy oil drain into an old can I found in the shack. As the flow lessened, it thickened. Eventually it stopped trickling out and fell in clumps, like when milk goes sour and turns into glue. I squeezed the oil between my fingers and felt the fine powder of the desert. It was amazing this engine had been able to run at all. Well, I would follow Ziegfried's directions. Then we would see.

I spent the whole day inside the shed, not coming out even once. Omar spent most of the day with me, which was a mixed blessing. At first, he stared over my shoulder with a kind of awe that reminded me of my watching Ziegfried, although Ziegfried was a master, I was just an apprentice. Eventually Omar got bored and kept trying to coax me outside to show me the mountainside, which I would have loved to see. But the thought of Seaweed sitting all alone beside the submarine made me work without stop. Then, unfortunately, Omar brought in his father's flute. How I wished he hadn't, because he couldn't play at all. He kept blowing into it, making the strangest, annoying sounds, and never seemed to tire of it. Half a dozen times I opened my mouth to ask him to stop, but couldn't quite get the words out. I didn't want to insult him. Maybe it was really important to him, I didn't know. I just thought he should stick to sponge diving; he was really good at that.

It was evening when I poured brand new, crystal-green oil into the old engine. I filled it up to the top and let it sit. I had cleaned out the filters, washed them with diesel fuel and let them evaporate dry. I had replaced the fuel line because the old one had looked like a cheap garden hose that someone had left outside for about twenty years. I cut a section from a longer hose that I brought, fit it and clamped it tight. Pumping fuel from the tank, I spun the flywheel and flicked the switch. There was a sound like a vacuum cleaner when the hose is plugged. "Rrrrrrrrrrrrr . . ." and then it died. Nothing. Then began my series of checks that would have made Ziegfried proud. I went over every part that could have possibly prevented the fuel from reaching its destination. I couldn't find anything. I tried to start it again — the same sound, then nothing. Omar's father and uncle came in and stared over my shoulder and nodded respectfully. As evening passed into night they asked if I would like to return to the tent to sleep. I thanked them and shook my head. I wouldn't have been able to sleep anyway. They brought me tea, went out, and a little while later I heard music.

I went over my checks again and again, with no success.

It was discouraging. How I wished I could have called Ziegfried. He would know right away what was wrong. I was tired. It was getting late. It was bothering me that I had left Seaweed alone for so long. In a fit of frustration, I yanked on the fuel line. Was it possible there was a hole inside of it and it was sucking air and preventing the diesel from passing through? It was just a wild guess. I unclamped the hose, let it drain, held it up to the light and looked through it. No, it was solid. I sat back down. I wasn't able to fix this engine. They had taken me into the desert for nothing.

I had to put the engine back the way it was and go outside and explain. It was not a very nice feeling. As I was re-clamping the fuel line I was also remembering the many times that Ziegfried had taught me something by intentionally creating a problem in the sub, so that it wouldn't work until I had found the problem and fixed it. It had been a very frustrating way to learn, for sure, but had taught me some invaluable lessons, in particular, to keep searching persistently. I decided to take one more look at the fuel injection system before going out to the men and admitting my failure.

Between the injector pump and the engine was the fuel injection line, but it was made of metal, not rubber. There were no holes in it and it was not leaking anywhere. The whole system was very simple, which was surely why it had lasted so long in the first place. At the very end of the injection line was a nozzle. I was surprised to discover this time that I could remove it. As I raised it up to the light, I couldn't believe what I saw. The hole in the nozzle, through which the fuel was supposed to pass, was almost sealed! In the way that a clam builds its shell — spinning coarse sand into smooth enamel — the fine powder of the desert, over many, many years, had closed in around the opening of the nozzle until it was virtually sealed shut. The fuel couldn't pass through!

I reached for my files, picked up the smallest one and scraped across the top of the opening, just until there was a hole big enough to pass the file through. Then I filed the hole carefully until it was brought back to its original size. I blew the powder away, wiped the nozzle with my shirt and reattached it to the line. I pumped the line with fuel, spun the flywheel and flicked the engine switch. "Rrrrrrrrrrrrr . . . rrrrrrrrrrrr . . . Rrrrroooooooaaaarrrrrrrr!" The diesel kicked into life. It was running! I was so happy! My grandfather's boat probably sounded better, but the engine was running. The men came rushing into the shed, yelling and saying blessings and hugging me. I heaved a heavy sigh of relief. In my heart, I thanked Ziegfried.

We prepared to leave in the morning. It took exactly the same amount of time to return. Camels are so slow and steady you can predict a journey with precision, which is important in crossing a desert. When the camels finally lumbered onto the beach, I jumped off, ran to the water and threw myself in. I swam straight to the old ship, where I found my first mate guarding the sub like the loyal sailor he was. It was a lonely sight, a lone seagull nestled down on the rusted-out shell of an ancient freighter. When he saw me he squawked loudly. I could tell he was glad to see me, although I wasn't sure if his squawk was a greeting or a complaint. He got fed right away in any case, and he deserved it — no one had stolen or vandalized the sub in our absence.

I was happy to be back at the seashore. The desert was fascinating for sure, but no place for a sailor. Omar's father wanted to give me a camel, as a way of saying thank you. It was a tremendous honour, though not exactly my first choice as a crew member. I suggested a present of oranges and dates instead, since they refused to let me leave empty-handed. It turned out to be a wonderful present; the oranges and dates filled the sub with freshness and sweetness.

After we said our goodbyes, the furry camels and their wrinkled masters returned to the burning heat of the desert. I watched them saunter off the beach and disappear into the vastness without so much as dipping a toe in the water. That seemed strange to me, that they wouldn't want to throw themselves into the sea after so much heat and dryness. Apparently not. I did manage to convince Omar to sail back to Jerba with me, where we spent the rest of the week diving for sponges, shooting pellet rifles and cooking over an open fire. It was so much fun. And yet my search for Atlantis was calling me. And so, with a promise to return on our way back home, I hugged my new friend, and we said goodbye for now. He left to sell his sponges and visit with his family; I gathered the crew and left the shores of Africa for Greece.

Chapter Twenty-four

೧௲

THEY WERE FLYING a white flag. As soon as I saw it I remembered Reggie's warning about pirates. But surely not everyone flying a white flag was a pirate? And yet I had to admit, I had a bad feeling about this one.

It was a wooden sailboat about thirty feet long, and had a rubber dinghy in tow with an outboard motor. I followed Reggie's advice and took a careful look at the boat through the binoculars, checking for any visible signs of damage. There were none. There hadn't been a storm. For all the time I had been in the Mediterranean it had been like sailing on a lake.

I had picked them up on radar first and was now peering at them from a mile away. It was doubtful they had seen us. I submerged to periscope level and motored closer. About a tenth of a mile away I had a pretty good look at them through the periscope. A man came out of the cabin and looked at something in a box. He was not distressed. He was kind of rough looking. But Reggie was rough looking, and he certainly wasn't a pirate. Then another man came out. He looked pretty much the same. Neither man appeared to be in trouble in any way. I had to wonder why they were in distress. Nobody was bailing. There was enough wind to sail. Surely if someone were sick or injured these two could sail for help. They also had the dinghy with the outboard motor, unless it was out of gas. Hmmm. It just didn't look right. And then I saw something that disturbed me. One of the men hit the other. And the other man didn't respond. He was afraid. Now I *knew* there was something wrong. The angry man started yelling at the timid man, and then a third man came out of the cabin, and he was even angrier than the second man. Now there were three men on deck, none of whom looked much like a sailor. I decided not to come to their assistance, which wasn't easy. When you were on the sea, you wanted to believe that anyone would stop and help you when you were in trouble. But my gut feeling was strong, and I was going to listen to it.

So, I sailed away and resurfaced. Reggie had also advised that I contact the authorities if I suspected there were pirates in the area. But I wasn't sure who to call. We were in the Sea of Crete now, in Greek waters, but weren't within the twelve-mile zone of any island. I decided to contact Ziegfried and ask his advice.

Ziegfried wasn't answering. Then I realized, he was probably already on his way over. I made myself a cup of tea and thought about it. Probably I should try to contact the authorities in Crete. I could identify myself as a Canadian sailor, without mentioning the sub, and describe everything else just as I had seen it.

I was about to make the call when I heard the radar beep. Another vessel was approaching the distressed sailboat from the other direction. We were now four miles away. The approaching vessel was five miles on the other side. Perhaps the stranded sailboat had called the authorities after all. Perhaps I had gotten it all wrong. On the other hand, what if the approaching vessel was an innocent sailboat coming to help and was going to be attacked by the pirates and its crew savagely killed? Yikes!

The approaching vessel wasn't very fast. That meant it probably wasn't the authorities. It must have been a sailboat. I had to go back.

The sailboat came in a straight line towards the distressed boat. They must have been using radar. I came in submerged, so that no one would know we were there, then rose to periscope level. The sailboat appeared. She was flying the Swedish flag — blue with a yellow cross. She was about the same size as the other boat and there were two people on deck, an older man and woman. They sailed closer, closer, closer . . . with the man on the bow trying to get a good look at the distressed boat. Suddenly, he yelled back to the woman who was at the helm, and she turned the wheel and brought their boat around. He had seen something he didn't like. The three men came running out of the cabin and two of them jumped into the dinghy, with machine guns! They were going to chase the other sailboat, which was now trying to get away!

The motorized dinghy wasn't very fast but it was only a matter of time before it would catch up to the fleeing sailboat. I surfaced so that the portal was just a foot above water, cranked up the engine and went after the dinghy. I didn't know what to do but had to do something. Then, I got an idea. I climbed inside and grabbed one of the pellet rifles and the last pack of pellets. The men in the dinghy were so focused on catching the sailboat I hoped they wouldn't turn around and see me chasing them. All they would have seen anyway would be my head sticking out of the portal and the waves caused by the movement of the sub. What I hoped to do was fire the whole packet of pellets into the rubber dinghy, and maybe it would sink.

As soon as I was within range I started shooting. They couldn't hear the pellet rifle and never turned around. But I couldn't tell if I was hitting the dinghy or not. I just aimed as well as I could and kept pumping and shooting the gun.

If they had ever turned around I would have slammed the hatch shut and dived. But they never did.

When all the pellets were gone, I submerged to periscope level again and continued the chase. The dinghy had almost caught the sailboat. I could see the men with machine guns laughing as the terrified couple tried to sail away, and then ... the dinghy started to slow down. It was deflating! It was going to sink! In a minute we were almost alongside the dinghy, just fifty feet away. But the pirates were scrambling around too much, trying to find out why they were sinking, to notice the periscope. I saw the couple in the sailboat reach for two lifebuoys. They were thinking of something I had failed to consider — maybe the pirates couldn't swim.

Well, one could, and one couldn't One of the two men started to swim back towards their own sailboat, which was slowly motoring to catch up. But he left his partner behind to fend for himself. The Swedish couple managed to throw a lifebuoy to him, and as soon as he grabbed it they let go of the rope. They wisely decided not to pull him to their own sailboat.

The pirate swimming back tried pathetically to keep his machine gun. He swam with one arm and held the gun above water with the other. But he soon grew tired and the gun slipped into the water. Then he wrapped it around his neck and tried to swim with two arms. Finally, he just let it sink. The other pirate clung to the lifebuoy with a look of panic. I hoped he would hold on. I didn't want him to drown, but I didn't want to rescue him either. I decided to stay and wait until the other pirates had rescued him. The other sailboat didn't. As they sailed away, they waved at the periscope! They had seen me!

When the two pirates picked up their mate, he immediately pointed to the periscope. He had spotted us too! The other two grabbed more machine guns and started firing at us! I flicked the dive switch and we went down, but not before I heard bullets bouncing off the hull. I wasn't afraid. I knew the bullets would lose their power as soon as they hit the water. From inside the sub, the bullets sounded like the tapping of a toy drum. Still, there was something very disturbing about being shot at. It made me angry. I was angry that they would turn the sea into such a dangerous place. I wasn't going to let them get away with it.

Chapter Twenty-five

WE CHASED THEM for a whole day. They seemed to be heading for North Africa, possibly Libya. They were terrible sailors. They couldn't seem to catch the wind properly, and when they did, by chance, they almost swamped their boat. After a while, they just gave up, dropped the sail and motored the rest of the way. But you can't motor endlessly in an old sailboat without running out of fuel. And they did.

I would much rather have been looking for Atlantis, and yet I couldn't let them get away. The Swedish couple must have called the authorities. Anyone who would answer a distress call and come to someone's rescue would surely call the authorities. However, the pirates had sailed away from that position. I decided to call in their present coordinates.

I contacted the Greek coastguard in Crete. They put me on to someone who spoke English.

"Identify your vessel and nationality . . ."

"I'm a Canadian sailor."

"Identify your vessel please."

"Umm . . . it's a sailboat."

"Please give your vessel registration number."

"That's not important. What's important is that there is a group of pirates out here waiting to catch somebody else."

"Please give your vessel registration number."

Shoot!

"I don't have one. Can I just give you the pirates' position, please?"

There was a long pause.

"Give the coordinates please."

I gave the coordinates, then I wanted to hang up. But they wouldn't let me go so easily.

"It is illegal to sail in Greece without an international vessel registration number. Please report your . . ."

I hung up. I wondered what they would have said if I told them my vessel was a submarine.

So I waited. I had been two days without sleep. The crew, of course, slept whenever they wanted to. But I was terribly sleepy, especially as we were just sitting still. Then, the wind picked up and the pirates were encouraged to try sailing again. I watched them through the periscope less than a quarter of a mile away. I wished the Greek coastguard would hurry up. I was falling asleep.

The wind was coming from the south and gaining strength quickly. I saw a dark orange cloud on the horizon, and I knew what *that* meant. I wondered if the pirates knew what it meant. I wondered if they knew enough to drop their sail.

Nope.

They seemed pleased to have the wind raise their sail so easily. For a little while they even managed to tack into the wind successfully. But the orange cloud hadn't hit with full strength yet. When it did, it struck the sailboat like a giant stepping on a blade of grass. The sailboat swamped and the pirates fell overboard. I surfaced, turned on the engine and motored closer, but kept the hatch closed. I was afraid Seaweed would take a chance and go out. I knew that at least one of the pirates couldn't swim and didn't know if the others would help him. Problem was, I couldn't see through the cloud, and I was worried that by the time I was close enough to see what was going on, one or more might have drowned.

When we finally approached, I saw three men clinging to the swamped boat. They saw the sub and waved frantically. What a bizarre situation! Normally, I would have hurried to their rescue. But I knew who they were and why they were here in the first place — they were thieves and probably murderers. If I rescued them, they would almost certainly steal my submarine and maybe even kill me, and Hollie and Seaweed. There was no way I would take that risk.

The wind continued to howl. I didn't know how long they could hold on, or, if their boat would even stay afloat. What would I do if it sank? Would I watch three men drown? I tried to prepare myself for that possibility but couldn't do it. There had to be a way; I just had to find it.

Eventually I came up with a plan. It might not have been the best plan, but it was better than nothing. First, I coaxed Seaweed to the portal, opened the hatch carefully and let him see the sandstorm. He immediately hopped back to the observation window and made himself cozy. I felt confident he would stay there. Then, I brought out the dinghy and lots of rope. I inflated the dinghy and tied several ten-foot lengths to its handles, so the pirates could tie themselves in. Then, I tied a hundred foot length of rope between the dinghy and the portal. I maneuvered in front of the capsized boat, facing into the wind, and let the dinghy go. One of the pirates grabbed hold of it and jumped in, then helped the others. I leaned against the portal and waited for them to tie themselves down. I was pretty sure that one of the pirates only pretended to tie himself to the dinghy, and I could guess why. He was planning to crawl along the rope to the sub when I wasn't looking.

I cranked up the engine and sailed into the wind. It surprised me that the pirates, so untrustworthy themselves, would be so quick to trust *me*. I supposed they didn't have much choice.

We were sailing towards Africa. But I had no intention of

docking, only of sailing within sight of land and setting the pirates adrift. I would throw them the paddles before I let them go. But we would enter the twelve-mile zone. Would that be in Libya or Egypt? I wasn't really sure.

I went back inside and pulled the hatch down without sealing it. Just as I had suspected, one of the pirates climbed onto the rope immediately. He didn't seem to realize that I could see him through the periscope. We were travelling at about fifteen knots and the wind was probably blowing at a hundred miles per hour. That was a lot of wind to fight when you were dragging yourself along a rope — in the sea! I watched him for a little while because it was so impossible and yet he was so determined. It was very funny. After ten minutes or so he had crawled almost halfway. But I could tell he was exhausted. I opened the hatch, strapped on the harness, stepped onto the stern and grabbed the rope. I lifted it up and gave it a quick snap. A wave went through the rope and hit him like a whip. But he held on. After three more whips he turned around and made a gesture for his companions to follow him, but neither of them would. I whipped the rope quickly three more times, he lost his grip and drifted back to the dinghy. As he climbed in, he tried to strike one of the other men but missed and slipped. I couldn't help laughing. I knew these men were very dangerous on land. At sea they were absolutely clueless.

In a few hours the wind had vanished and it was dark. The sky was clear once again and the stars glittered. I saw distant lights from shore before we picked up anything on radar. We had just entered the twelve-mile zone. I still wasn't sure if it was Egypt or Libya. We weren't hanging around either way. Five miles from shore I shot a long flare, a short one, and another long one. I waited. Fifteen minutes later, radar revealed two vessels leaving shore and heading towards us. I untied the rope. I was sorry to lose so much rope and a dinghy that had served us so well, but couldn't see any other way. We could pick up more rope and a new dinghy in Crete. Once I saw the lights of the approaching vessels, I shut the hatch, dove to two hundred feet and we disappeared. I would have liked to warn the local authorities about what was waiting for them in the dinghy but couldn't risk losing the sub.

They would figure it out.

Chapter Twenty-six

IT WAS AS IF someone had lit a giant firecracker beneath the island of Thera in 1500 BC, and blew it up. The firecracker was a volcano, and it was still active.

The last eruption was in 1956, but there were always gasses escaping from the ground, which made beautiful sunsets for the tourists, and Thera had lots of tourists! You would know when the island was going to blow, they said, when the water started getting murky.

We sailed in at night, on the surface, without lights or flags. I wanted to make as careful a reconnaissance as possible before finding a place to sleep. Thera had once been a small island with a mountain in the center, like a cupcake.

Now it was a doughnut with a couple of bites missing, and you could sail right inside the perimeter and around the smaller pieces sticking up here and there. It was very rocky, but not like any other island I had ever seen. The sand was black! The rock was volcanic, with hard-packed ash on top of it, layer upon layer, which all looked like it was going to collapse any second. On top of that were built villages of shiny white houses, white churches and bright blue roofs, all lit up at night like candles. It was very pretty. There were no trees, grass or bushes anywhere, just jagged rocky cliffs, with villages clinging like bird nests. The bay was packed with yachts and sailboats, none of them sitting at anchor; it was too deep. They were moored to buoys linked by chains. The volcano had blown a hole under the water too, all the way down to 1500 feet! Was Atlantis down there?

We motored silently through the shadows and dark corridors of the island, between the cliffs and moored boats, until I began to get my bearings. Then, we submerged to two hundred feet and I studied the sonar screen. The terrain was even stranger beneath the sea. But I could only bounce sonar waves off it; I couldn't get close enough to see it. Outside of the island, around the perimeter, the sea floor was only a hundred feet deep in places. We glided over it in the darkness and the sonar revealed some very peculiar patterns. I wanted to hit the floodlights and have a look but was afraid someone might see the lights from the cliffs, or from a boat. I would just have to wait and explore in the daylight. In the meantime, we would catch some sleep. Before the sunrise I sailed to the far side of one of the tiny isolated islands, submerged to two hundred feet and went to sleep. I was pretty sure it was uninhabited because it was just a rock.

In the late afternoon we surfaced. I opened the hatch and climbed out with Hollie. Standing on the very edge of the little island, with her hands on her hips as if she had been waiting for twenty years to get off, was the most surprised and angriest woman I had ever seen.

"Who . . . what . . . where . . . how did you . . . ? Who are you? And what do you think you are doing?"

She was *really* angry. Talk about a volcano!

Her name was Penelope Sargeant. She was professor of archaeology at the University of Chicago. She spent a lot of time on the island of Thera, she said, because her specialty was Atlantis. She had written a book about it. I had read it.

"You're not allowed to be down there, doing that! Don't you know you aren't allowed . . . don't you know it is forbidden to . . . how did you get here anyway . . . how . . . you . . . you'd better get the heck out of here before I call the police!"

Then Seaweed dropped out of the sky, landed on the hatch beside me, opened his beak and squawked for breakfast.

"Just a minute," I said, and went inside the sub. When I came out, I threw Seaweed some dog biscuits. Penelope was still standing there with her mouth open. There was no one else on the little island.

"Did . . . did you just feed a seagull?"

"Yes."

"But . . . wait . . . is that a submarine?"

"Yes."

Penelope sat down and started rubbing her forehead. I wondered if maybe she had been in the sun too long, she looked so upset.

"Look, young man. What's your name?"

"Alfred."

"Where are you from?"

"Newfoundland."

She peeked out from behind her hands.

"You're from Newfoundland?"

"Yes."

"How did you get here?"

"We sailed here."

"Oh my gosh . . . that's unbelievable . . . that's . . . who's *we*?"

"Seaweed — that's him, and Hollie."

I held Hollie up for her to see.

"This is my crew."

"A seagull and a dog?"

"Yes."

She started to laugh.

"I must be going crazy!"

Maybe. I didn't really care. If she were going to report us, we would just sail away. But first, I had promised Hollie a walk, and he was going to get one, whether she liked it or not. I moored the sub to the rock and we jumped over. There wasn't much beach to speak of but he could run around on the rock. Penelope just sat quietly for a while and watched us. Then she got up and followed us.

"Don't you realize it is forbidden to dive in Greek waters, which are all archaeologically sensitive areas?"

"Yes, but I'm not diving, I'm just sailing."

"But you're in a submarine."

"So?"

"So . . . you're under the water."

"So?"

She took a deep breath but didn't answer. Hollie found a stick and brought it to me. I pretended to hide it, then threw it for him.

"Look, Alfred. I've spent my whole life studying and searching for Atlantis. These are delicate places of great historical importance; you can't just come barging in here like you're some kind of treasure hunter, and disturb the sites."

"I'm not a treasure hunter, and I'm not disturbing the sites."

"Then what are you?"

"An explorer."

"Oh."

She was quiet again for a while. I could tell she was thinking really hard about something.

"What are you exploring for, Alfred?"

"Lots of things. I just love exploring. Right now I'm look-ing for Atlantis."

"So you *are* looking for Atlantis? You can't just jump into the water and go looking for Atlantis. You have to study it. It's very, very complicated. There are centuries of informa-tion to go through. There are theories, scientific evidence and archaeological sites to consider."

"I know."

"What do you mean, you know? How old are you?"

"Fifteen."

"You're fifteen? And you've sailed across the world in a submarine?"

"I've studied too."

"Oh? *Have* you? Which universities have you attended?"

Penelope was starting to bug me.

"Well? Answer me. What studying have you done?"

I felt like telling her I had read her book and that it wasn't any good.

"I'm an explorer, not an archaeologist."

I also felt like pointing out that she and I were standing in the same place, but that should have been obvious to her.

"Look. Alfred. Just by coming through here with your sub-marine you might have disturbed the delicate balance of things under the water. There's a huge mound of broken houses and pottery and sunken statues just offshore in shal-lower waters."

"Rows, actually."

"No, it's a big mound."

"There isn't one big mound, just a bunch of smaller rows, like waves."

"Excuse me. It clearly says in my texts that the shallower waters outside of Thera contain a large mound of ancient debris, *not rows*! I think I know what I'm talking about!"

I stared at her. She was probably fifty years old. She looked kind of old and young at the same time. She was lean, had long dark hair with gray streaks, very tanned skin and lots of wrinkles. She had a friendly face, actually, but looked sort of burnt out, as if her many years of searching for Atlantis had exhausted her. Now she was arguing with me about something I had just seen, which she had only read about in a book. There was something so pointless about it all.

"Okay."

"You see? It's just one large mound. Right?"

"Yup."

"Good."

Whatever. After Hollie had a good run-around we headed back to the sub. Penelope just stood there and watched us go, but she looked upset. She seemed to have a painful argument going on inside her head. She looked so alone on the little island, just her and her research. I felt kind of sorry for her.

"Good luck!" I called out, as we climbed into the sub.

She stared without answering. I even wondered if she were going to cry.

"Wait!" she hollered.

I poked my head up from the portal.

"Yah?"

"Ummm, you sailed from Newfoundland, right?"

"Right."

"So, your submarine is safe, right?"

"Right."

She came over, looked around to see if anyone was watching — took several deep breaths and . . .

"I'm *really* not supposed to do this but do you think maybe you could give me a ride?"

Chapter Twenty-seven

✍

I TOOK PENELOPE down to a hundred and fifty feet and made her a cup of tea. She settled on a pillow beside the observation window. Hollie sat beside her and looked up at her wistfully, but she wasn't too interested in him. We cruised outside the perimeter of Thera, hovering between one hundred and three hundred feet. Once we were under water Penelope seemed to forget completely about the rule of no diving in the Greek islands. And it was a little like taking your teacher out to play — she was bossy!

"Go here, Alfred! Go here! Go over there! Go up here! Go down there! Stop here! Go back! Go *back*!!"

At one point, she even reached for the controls, but I blocked her.

"You'd better not do that," I said. "It's not as easy as it looks."

As wild as Thera looked above water, it was stranger underneath. There were deep holes in the sea floor caused by volcanic eruptions. The holes were surrounded by perfectly round rings of soil, like giant ant holes — their centers disappearing into who knows where. Besides the rings of soil were long rows of debris, like huge waves in a city dump. It was exciting, for sure, but it really did look like a dump. It might have been a dump from the amazing city of Atlantis . . . but it was still a dump. I couldn't imagine anyone digging this stuff up and sorting through it. It would take hundreds of years! But that's exactly where Penelope got really excited.

"Oh my gosh! Look at that! Oh! Look! There's an urn! Stop! Alfred! Stop! There's an urn! Wait! What's that? Is that a boat? Alfred, is that a boat? How old do you suppose it is?"

"I don't know. Could be fifty years old. Could be five hundred. It's hard to tell."

"Hmm . . . what's that?"

I stared down through the observation window.

"Looks like a big plate."

"What do you think it's made of?"

"I don't know. It's hard to say. When things have been on the bottom for a while they get covered with sea muck and you can't even tell if they're made of metal or wood."

"I think it's made of metal. Look."

I looked again. It looked like a plastic saucer I used to slide down the hill with when I was little. Penelope's eyes grew wider.

"It looks like a shield to me."

I didn't think it was a shield.

"I think it's a shield, Alfred. Oh, my gosh!"

"Umm . . . I don't think . . ."

"Do you have any idea how important that would be?"

"Yes, but . . ."

"Oh! Alfred, is there any way you can pick up things with your submarine?"

"No."

"Shoot!"

I took a deep breath. I didn't know if it were a good idea or not, but . . .

"But I can dive down there. It's just a hundred feet."

"What do you mean?"

"I mean: I can free-dive to a hundred feet."

"You mean . . . you can *swim* down there?"

"Yes."

"But it's so far."

"I know, but I can. But we're not supposed to touch any-thing."

"I know, I know, but maybe you could just swim down and take a closer look at that shield. Maybe you could very gently turn it over."

I had to confess, the thought that it might be an ancient shield *was* pretty exciting, although if I had been listening to my own gut feeling then I wouldn't have gone down. But Penelope was absolutely convinced it was an important find. I brought the sub awash, the portal sticking up just a foot above the surface. Even like that we were risking being spotted by someone from the cliffs. I climbed out, did my deep breathing and went down.

The water was clear and beautiful. I was surprised how easy it was to reach one hundred feet. Sponge diving with Omar had improved my skills. I found the round object and pulled it free. It was made of metal for sure but was very light. I didn't think it was a shield. I looked up at the sub but couldn't see Penelope in the observation window. Back on the surface she stuck her head out the portal.

"Why don't you just bring it up so we can have a look at it, Alfred? Then we'll put it back."

So, I went back down, grabbed it and brought it up. I was pretty sure it was a plate. Penelope reached down and took it from me as I climbed up. Very excitedly, she rubbed the sea muck off it.

"You were right, Alfred, it's a plate. But look, it's cut in re-lief. There are figures of warriors fighting. Look! A bull! That means it's Minoan. The bull is a symbol of the Minoan civ-ilization."

"How old do you think it is?"

"I don't know. If it's made of bronze, then it's very old.

But it seems too light to be bronze. It might be brass. Oh, wait! There's a stamp."

"A stamp? What does it say?"

Penelope squinted.

"Wait. I need my glasses."

She pulled old-fashioned glasses out of her shirt pocket and read the stamp and burst out laughing.

"What's so funny?"

"It says, 'Made in China.'"

"Oh."

"It probably just fell off a cruise ship."

Penelope handed the plate back to me, meaning, I guessed, that I should get rid of it. Well, I wasn't going to swim down and put it back exactly where it had been, if it was worthless, although maybe in a thousand years it would be valuable, and people would be amazed that it came all the way from China. I tossed it into the sea and watched it sink. Penelope's mood changed.

"Oh, well, that was silly. I'm surprised at myself for getting so worked up. It's going to be dark soon. Do you think you could take me back to where I was?"

"Sure."

So, we went back down. Penelope took her seat at the observation window again. A few minutes later she saw something else.

"Alfred?"

"Yah?"

"Can you come and look at this?"

I stopped the sub. She was pointing at something and her face looked shocked. I came over.

"What," she said, "do you suppose *that* is?"

I took a peek.

"It looks like an arm to me."

"It is, isn't it?"

She looked up at me like a child who really wanted something.

"Do you think you could dive down and take a look?"

I stared at the arm sticking up from the bottom. It looked kind of creepy. But I was curious too.

"Yah, I guess so."

We surfaced and I went down. It was getting dark so I brought a waterproof flashlight. At first I couldn't find the arm, and then there it was, as if it were reaching up to grab me. I touched it. It felt like stone. I moved some of the debris away from it. The arm was connected to a head and part of a torso. I tried to get a good look but had to surface.

"Well?" said Penelope.

"It's part of a statue."

"Does it seem really old?"

"Yah, I think so."

"Oh my gosh!"

"I'll go back down."

This time I got a pretty good look at the face. It was a beautiful young woman. She was probably made of marble or something like that. There was just the upper part of the body, and only one arm. I felt around for other pieces but didn't find any. I had to surface.

"Well? Well? What did you see?"

I described everything.

"Could you lift it?"

"No way, it's too heavy. You would have to raise it with a rope."

Penelope looked all around the sub. "Do . . . you . . . *have* a rope?"

So I went back down with a rope, tied it around the broken torso and swam back up. Carefully, we raised it. I did the pulling and Penelope wrapped the rope around the portal, in case it slipped from my hands. For only part of a statue, it was really heavy. When we brought it alongside the sub, it was almost dark. Penelope was extremely excited. She clapped her hands together.

"Oh my gosh! Oh my gosh! Oh my gosh!"

"Shhhhhh!"

I wanted her to be quiet because people might hear us on the water.

"I'm sorry! I'm just so excited. Oh my gosh, it's ancient! I can't believe it!"

We raised the statue out of the water but it would not fit through the portal.

"Quick, Alfred! Take me back to the little island. I will say I found it there."

"Really? But that's just a rock. How will you explain how it got there?"

"There's a little sandy spot on one side. I'll say I found it there, just under the water. I'll say . . . I stumbled on it there."

It was completely dark when we returned to the spot where I first met Penelope. It took both of us to carry the statue and put it down on the little sandy spot. Then it seemed to take forever to position it so that it looked like Penelope had just found it. If ever there was a time that I felt like a real outlaw . . . this was it.

Penelope was all over the statue like a dog with a bone. She seemed to forget I was even there.

"Do you think it might be from Atlantis?" I asked.

"What? Oh . . . maybe. It's *very* beautiful, isn't it? We don't have any statues of this size from the Minoan period, only frescoes. If it *is* Minoan, well, then, maybe it could be from Atlantis. We'll have to date it of course, and . . ."

She drifted away in thought. It was time for us to leave. I didn't want to get caught. I coaxed Seaweed onto the sub.

"I think we're going to go now."

I wasn't sure if she had heard me. "Good luck!" I called out.

"What? Oh. Oh, good luck, Alfred! Happy sailing! Thank you! Thank you!"

"You're welcome."

I wondered if she had really found a piece of Atlantis. I knew one thing for sure: if the sea beneath Thera *were* the ancient site of Atlantis, it was now nothing but a dump. And it would take a lot more than a few archaeologists to reconstruct it. As Penelope disappeared into the dark, we waved one last time. I couldn't help wondering if being a professor of archaeology was not really her thing. Maybe she should have been a treasure hunter.

Chapter Twenty-eight

SOMETIMES, WHEN YOU can't explain what is happening around you, it feels like you are drifting through a dream. Everything you thought you knew about the world and how it works is challenged, and that can be kind of scary. But if you don't let that fear get the best of you, it can also be pretty exciting.

We had left Penelope on her rock, wrestling with the beautiful statue in the sand. We were sailing towards Crete, only seventy-five miles south. It was a moonless night and very dark. Darkness on the sea always seems darker than on land. But the sea was calm, and Hollie and I were leaning against the hatch, watching the stars, which were sparkling more than usual in the absence of the moon. We were cruising at sixteen knots when I thought I heard a beep. I listened for a second one. There wasn't one.

"Did you hear that, Hollie?"

Hollie looked up at me, wanting to please.

"Did you hear the radar beep?"

He squinted and looked around in the darkness and sniffed the midnight air. I yawned.

"Oh, well, I suppose we should go in and take a peek. It's probably nothing."

I climbed inside, put Hollie down and went to the radar screen. The radar swept its wave around the screen but nothing lit up and nothing beeped. I stared for a few minutes, yawning, and was about to go back outside when the sonar screen caught my eye. The sea floor between Thera and Crete was deep, between six and seven thousand feet, but the sonar was showing three hundred.

"That can't be right."

I reached for my charts. No, there was no indication of an underwater ridge between Thera and Crete. I stared at the sonar screen, then watched wide-eyed as the sea floor rapidly fell from three hundred to six thousand feet. The numbers dropped so quickly it was like falling off a mountain. I grabbed my charts again and pored over them very carefully.

"No. No, there's nothing there."

I stared back at the sonar screen. The sea floor was sixty-two hundred feet below us. Five minutes later it was still the same.

"Whoa! Wait! Okay, what's going on?"

I stopped the sub. Hollie barked and wagged his tail. He could feel my excitement.

"Let's go back, Hollie. I want to check that depth again."

I turned the sub around and headed back the way we had come. Watching the sonar screen the whole time, I waited to see the sea floor rise. Five minutes passed, ten minutes, fifteen, but the sea floor stayed the same. I stopped the sub, climbed out and looked around. Seaweed was sitting on the bow.

"Hi, Seaweed. Just checking our depth."

Seaweed didn't see any food in my hands so he didn't care.

I went back inside, looked at the charts once more and stared at the sonar. The sea floor was well over a mile down. Was it possible the sonar had malfunctioned? Was it possible a very large submarine had passed slowly beneath us at three hundred feet? But that wouldn't explain the mountain-like wall I had seen on the screen. I shrugged, started the engine and sat down to watch the sonar screen as we sailed over the area once again. Ten minutes later the radar beeped. Something was outside, right beside us! I raced up the portal, looked around in the darkness for a light or something, but there was nothing. The radar beeped again. I rushed back inside. The sonar indicated a depth of three hundred feet. I reached for the switch and cut the engine. We drifted slowly to a stop. Then, from the observation window came a faint blue glow. There was light underneath the sub! My mouth dropped. Something about the light was weird. It wasn't bright and yet it was sparkling, like stars. I didn't rush now; I was too mystified. I went to the portal and climbed up the ladder. Part of me wanted to look, and part wanted to hit the engine switch and sail away as fast as possible.

I raised my head out of the portal and saw a shiny blue light in the water all around us. At a glance, the light had a radius of about a quarter of a mile. It was such a strange light. It didn't seem to be coming from any one spot, but from everywhere. I had the strange sense that the light was somehow lifting us up in the air. But it wasn't. Certainly the space occupied by the light was far too big for it to be any kind of human-made object. Besides, it wasn't really a light as much as a glow. Suddenly, I thought maybe I knew what it was! Luminescence! I had read about strange sightings at sea of weird light phenomena that were caused by a special kind of algae. The blue glow could be coming from billions and billions of tiny algae, each emitting its own little luminescent energy.

This was a comforting theory. I started to relax. The blue glow was very beautiful to look at. It was almost a mirror of the stars. It was the most mysterious thing I had ever seen.

But a luminescence didn't explain the sonar reading. I went back inside and looked at the screen — three hundred feet. That was impossible. I wished I had a depth cable that I could lower three hundred feet and see if it touched bottom. I started the engine and slowly sailed out of the luminescence, and as we left the glow, the sea floor dropped to sixty-two hundred feet once more. Darkness surrounded us. Well, at least I could tell that the luminescence seemed to be causing the bizarre change in depth. But then I remembered that on our first trip over the area, the sonar read three hundred feet and there had been no glow in the water. Neither had we encountered three hundred feet on our way back. I was confused. Was it that we'd only see the luminescence when we were sailing slowly or were stopped? I turned around and went back slowly, fully expecting to see the lovely blue glow. But it was gone. The sonar revealed a sea floor sixty-two hundred feet below.

"This is crazy!"

I turned around and went over the area again. No sign of luminescence and no change in depth. Perhaps we had drifted west with the current. I crossed the area again, correcting for a small amount of lateral drift. Nope. Nothing.

By the last hour of darkness we had crossed the area a dozen times and found nothing more. I was beginning to wonder if my mind had been playing tricks on me all along. And then something happened that sent a shiver right up my spine.

There was a splash outside and a thumping on the stern, as if something heavy had come out of the water and landed on the hull. Then, it took what felt like a step, and then another one. I froze. I held my breath and listened. It was absolutely silent.

"Seaweed?" I called.

The thought that Seaweed was out there by himself made me move towards the ladder. Then something jumped from the hull, and there was another splash. I climbed the portal and stuck my head out. There was nothing on the stern. When I turned and looked at the bow, Seaweed was gone!

There was something in the water. I could sense it. It's just a feeling you get, like something is staring at you. And then, I heard it. It came straight towards the sub, racing through the water like lightning. It jumped . . . and went right over my head! It came so close that I could have reached out and touched its tail. Now I knew what it was. I flicked on the sub's floodlights and swept them across the water. Dolphins! The sea was full of them.

I smiled. Dolphins are really smart. And they like to play. I couldn't help wondering if they thought the sub was some kind of "dummy" dolphin, with our new nose and paint. Maybe they wanted to play with us. Hollie whined at the bottom of the ladder. He wanted to come up. I went down, picked him up and carried him up the portal. His belly was already vibrating like a tiny motor and his teeth were chattering with the quietest growl imaginable. It always sounded like he wanted to growl but didn't want anyone to know he was doing it. I doubted that a herd of dolphins was going to be afraid.

Then, Hollie surprised me. He barked. It was a brave attempt to defend his territory. He was used to barking at seals in the boathouse. Maybe he thought these were seals in the water. The dolphins started calling back. Their calls were like soft screams. They were friendly. Hollie barked a few more times and the dolphins screamed back. Then there was a different sound, but it wasn't a dolphin. It was also a kind of scream but it wasn't soft or particularly friendly. It came from further away. It was a strange and frightening sound; I had never heard anything like it.

Holding Hollie tightly in one arm, I turned the flood-lights toward the scream. The water was tossing with move-ment. Silhouettes of dolphins crisscrossed in front of the light but it was very hard to see anything else. Suddenly, a dolphin came sailing through the air and went over our heads. Splashes of water fell on us. I grabbed the floodlights and spun them back. As they cut an arc through the water they passed over something unbelievable. I mean, I saw it . . . but I didn't believe it.

My eyes were playing tricks on me. I swung the lights again. Four or five dolphins were racing towards us. They were diving in and out of the water and picking up speed. I couldn't coordinate the lights well enough to follow them but all of the dolphins went over us, and something was rid-ing on the back of one of them. It just couldn't be what I thought it was . . . It looked like a little boy.

My mind raced. I knew what Sheba would say, because she believed in mermaids. Well, I didn't believe it could be a boy riding a dolphin, and so I tried to figure out what else it could be.

Dolphins, like fish, are always in danger of swimming into

garbage in the water — plastic rings and things like that. Sometimes they get trapped in them and drown, which is really sad. Sometimes they are able to swim away, and they carry the garbage attached to their bodies for the rest of their lives, or, sadly, until it slowly strangles them. Was that what I had seen, a piece of plastic wrapped around the body of a dolphin so that it looked like a little boy?

That was a good answer. It made sense. It made me feel better. But something was nagging me. And I knew what it was.

Darkness was fading. The water grew calm. The dolphin herd had moved on as quickly as they had appeared. I looked up in the sky for Seaweed but it was still too dark to see him. Then I saw something lying on the back of the stern, something small. Putting Hollie down inside, I strapped on the harness and climbed out onto the stern. I picked up the object. It was a small branch from an olive tree. There were three leaves on it. How strange. Then Seaweed dropped out of the sky.

"Hi, Seaweed. Did you drop this?"

He shook his beak. He probably did. He loved to pick things off the water and drop them in the sub. I looked around in the growing dawn. Inside of me a question was burning to get out, to shout to the sea all around me. And yet I couldn't even say it out loud. I was afraid. But I could think it.

Were we in Atlantis?

Chapter Twenty-nine

⌀

THE FIRST PERSON I saw on the island of Crete stood like a giant on the pier. He had a large head of wooly hair, huge shoulders and arms and looked like he could wrestle a bull into the ground. He must have intimidated the local people just by walking through their villages. If it were ancient times they would certainly have written an epic or two about him. Of course it was Ziegfried.

I got teary-eyed when I saw him; I couldn't help it. He looked a little different though, dressed in touristy clothes and wearing his tough look, which said, "Don't mess with me!" No one ever would, that was for sure. But if you looked closely, his t-shirt revealed another side of him, which I had come to know so well. On the front was a picture of a puppy and kitten, which must have been given to him by Sheba, and which he would therefore wear, no matter what. Beneath the picture were the words, "Endangered Species!" I laughed.

"Al!" he shouted, and lunged towards me and gave me one of his great bear hugs. Then he couldn't speak for a few minutes because he was so emotional. He reached down instead and picked up Hollie, and then his tears really started to fall. He looked up into the sky with a questioning face.

"He's around here somewhere," I said, wiping my face. That was enough crying for a couple of men, it seemed to me.

We walked off the pier and down along the beach. Snow-capped mountains rose majestically above lush green forests, olive orchards and orange groves. It was semi-tropical.

"Where did you hide the sub?"

"Behind a rock, on the northwestern tip of the island. We swam to the main island."

"Swam? Why didn't you take the dinghy?"

"Ummm . . . that's a long story."

"I'm sure it is. Don't spare me the details, I want to hear everything."

I was nervous telling Ziegfried *everything*. Usually I'd leave out certain things, the dangerous things, such as being shot at. I was afraid that if I told him exactly how dangerous it was sometimes, he wouldn't want me to continue. And yet, walking on the beach together in Crete, and being treated so respectfully by him, as he had always treated me . . . I felt he deserved nothing less than to hear the whole story. And so I told him, and left nothing out.

We walked all the way down the beach, across a breakwater and down another long beach. Ziegfried listened carefully, only interrupting when he needed to hear something twice. When I finished, he was quiet for a long time. I waited anxiously, wondering what he was thinking, wondering what he was going to say. He surprised me.

"Your grandparents send you their love," he said.

"Oh. Thanks."

"Sheba does too, of course."

"Thanks."

He picked up a flat rock and skipped it on the water. The rock skipped about twelve times before it sank. I had no idea he could skip rocks.

"So . . . what do you think of my story?"

He took a deep breath and sighed.

"You live a dangerous life, Al."

I shrugged my shoulders. "It's not so dangerous."

"You're an outlaw. That's a dangerous life."

"I don't want to be an outlaw. I just want to explore. It's just that . . ."

I looked over at Ziegfried. He was trying to pull a stick from Hollie's mouth. Hollie wouldn't give up a stick for anyone, not even Ziegfried. He lifted Hollie into the air and still he wouldn't let go.

"Yah, I guess I am."

"Everything we do has consequences, Al. As long as you're prepared to accept the consequences of your actions, and don't hurt anybody, you can do what you want."

"I am prepared to accept the consequences."

"I know you are. That's what makes you a man."

I liked that answer. And yet I was never so uncertain about myself as I was just then, ever since the events of the other night.

"So what do you think about what I saw?"

Ziegfried turned and looked at me and he had the same slightly pained look on his face that I had — the look of not wanting to believe in something crazy, but not knowing what else to think.

"I don't know, Al. Your theory about plastic trapped around the dolphin makes sense to me. So does the phosphorescence. Those things really happen. Maybe the phosphorescence was responsible for the variation in depth readings."

"But what about the weird, awful screeching?"

"Maybe that same dolphin was making a different sound because of the restriction the plastic was causing."

That seemed a pretty reasonable explanation too. And yet my skin tingled whenever I remembered the sound. Sheba had described the singing of mermaids just like that. So had

Reggie. And my efforts to convince myself that what I had seen was plastic, not a little boy, were not really successful.

"But how do I explain all of that happening at the same time, at the same place?"

"Well, you can call it coincidence, I suppose, but it strikes me that the dolphins might have been just as amazed by the phosphorescence as you were."

"Oh. Yah. That makes sense."

The more I talked to Ziegfried about it, the more I began to think that I had not been in the neighborhood of Atlantis at all, at least not a *living* Atlantis. And yet, I knew that if I were talking with Sheba, the conclusions would be completely different. That would come later.

But that wasn't the end of it. We rented a car and drove to the palace of King Minos, one of the centers of the ancient Minoan civilization. It had been destroyed by earthquakes and volcanoes and had lain in a pile of rubble for thousands of years. Archaeologists had been rebuilding it for almost a hundred. The palace *itself* was a maze. Ziegfried couldn't get his head around it because it had been built without symmetry. We walked through it for hours and he got really worked up about it.

"Al, you've got to understand, symmetry is like religion to architecture, especially ancient architecture. Look at the ancient temples everywhere else — they're as evenly balanced as a two-bladed ax! There's no symmetry here! None whatsoever! This is unbelievable!"

I had to smile. Ziegfried could explain away all the unbelievable things I had seen and yet he was stumped when it came to the way a building had been put together. But there was something else waiting for us around the corner. We turned . . . and there were the frescoes.

"Oh!"

They were large, colourful paintings on stone walls. The people, the ancient Minoans, were beautiful, just like the statue Penelope had found. They were a tall, elegant people, well-dressed and intelligent looking. There was something very strangely modern about them. Then we saw a fresco of a huge bull, with athletes leaping over it. And then we saw frescoes of dolphins. And there were people swimming with them. And there were people *riding* them.

We stared for a long time without saying a word. Even Hollie stared, and growled a little bit. I knew Ziegfried's brain was busy trying to make sense of it all. Finally, he broke the silence.

"Well, . . . they swim with dolphins in aquariums, don't they?"

"Yup."

They did.

Epilogue

⁂

IF ATLANTIS WAS part of the Minoan civilization, which I
believed it probably was, I had a better idea now why people
were still talking about it. It was such an amazing civilization to begin with. They were so advanced they even had hot
and cold running water and flushing toilets — four thousand years ago! They had a unique and unusual way of looking at the world. For instance, they never built walls to pro-
tect their cities from invaders. Why was that? Did they have
a secret weapon? Did they know something their enemies
didn't? Some people have suggested the people of Atlantis
knew terrible catastrophes were coming their way and prepared for them by developing a way of living under water,

beneath a giant bubble, or even developing gills! I laughed
when I read that, then was shocked that Ziegfried didn't. It
wasn't as far-fetched as it sounded, he said. Gills and lungs
function basically the same way — they isolate oxygen mol-
ecules and pump them into the blood. Lungs take oxygen
from air; gills take it from water. It was even conceivable to
breathe under water with lungs, he said, if you could find a
way to fill the water with enough oxygen. That sounded
pretty crazy to me, but so did landing on the moon, probably, until it was done. We have artificial lungs today, Ziegfried said, and organ transplants, test-tube babies, cloning
and all kinds of weird things. What would our scientists and
inventors come up with today if they had to prepare for a
giant meteor crashing into the earth? Yikes!

But did that mean I had to believe in mermaids now and
children riding around on dolphins at sea? No way. Not yet.
But I did understand Reggie's words a little better, that the
longer he was at sea, the more he felt he was not alone. Still,
Atlantis had been lost for thousands of years; I was only fifteen. I was just getting started.

We spent a couple of weeks exploring Crete. We visited
temples, monasteries, museums, caves, markets, villages and
junkyards. We went hiking in the mountains and swimming
in the sea. On our last day we restocked the sub with food
and fuel and bought more rope and a new dinghy. We said
goodbye in the twilight on an isolated rock, and Ziegfried

went to catch the night ferry back to Athens. I picked up Hollie and we climbed into the sub. We submerged to periscope depth, waited for the ferry and followed it out. A few miles from shore we surfaced behind the ship. I didn't care if anyone saw us but I knew Ziegfried would be watching. I climbed the portal and waved. Ziegfried waved back and saluted. We would meet again in just a few months at Sheba's, but for now my journey would continue. As I stood up on the portal and saluted back, I noticed a young girl standing next to Ziegfried. She waved too. She had seen us. Then Seaweed sailed out of the sky, tapped his beak on the hatch and dropped inside. I wondered how that must have looked to the little girl. Would it change the way she looked at the world?

The radar beeped. I climbed inside. Two vessels were coming our way from shore.

"Time to go, guys!" I said to the crew.

I shut the hatch, submerged to two hundred feet . . . and we disappeared.

ABOUT THE AUTHOR

 Philip Roy hails from Antigonish, Nova Scotia, and has a deep affection for the sea, having grown up beside it and lived by it on different shores. His university studies included music and history, but he has always wanted to write novels. *Submarine Outlaw*, his first book, grew out of a life-long fascination with submarines. *Journey to Atlantis* is the product of another dream — to work with myths and legends from the world's great literature. "These are the stories we grow up with and live with all our lives," says Philip. He is already busy on the next book in the *Submarine Outlaw* series.

MARQUIS

Québec, Canada

RECYCLED
Paper made from
recycled material
FSC® C103567

Printed on Enviro 100% post-consumer EcoLogo certified paper,
processed chlorine free and manufactured using biogas energy.

100%   PERMANENT